Stacey's Problem

Ann M. Martin

AN
APPLE
PAPERBACK

SCHOLASTIC INC.
New York Toronto London Auckland Sydney
Mexico City New Delhi Hong Kong

The author gratefully acknowledges
Suzanne Weyn
for her help in
preparing this manuscript.

ISBN 0-590-52345-7

12 11 10 9 8 7 6 5 4 3 2 1 0 1 2 3 4 5/0

Printed in the U.S.A. 40

First Scholastic printing, June 2000

Chapter 1

"Anchovies! Ew, no way!" I cried. I couldn't believe Mom was actually thinking of putting those smelly little fish on our beautiful homemade pizza. "Put them away, please," I begged her.

Mom looked down longingly at the oval tin of anchovies she held. She turned to my friend Claudia Kishi for support. "Do you like anchovies, Claudia?"

Claudia wrinkled her nose and shook her head so fiercely that her long black hair fanned out around her shoulders.

"How about putting them on just my third of the pie?" Mom suggested.

Claudia's lips twitched as she considered this. "That's fair," she agreed.

I sighed. I just *knew* the anchovy juice was going to contaminate the rest of the pizza. Which was so unfair. We'd spent nearly two hours on this pizza, ever since Claudia and I had come in from our Friday BSC meeting.

BSC is short for Baby-sitters Club. We call it a club because all the members are friends, but it's really more of a baby-sitting business. We meet three times a week in Claudia's room. Clients call during meetings to hire sitters. That way they can reach a bunch of sitters with one phone call.

When we returned to my house after the meeting, Mom was already working on the pizza dough. Right away, we began helping her with it. We took turns pounding it, then letting it rise, then pounding it again. Over and over.

All the while, Mom's special tomato sauce simmered on the stove. She doesn't make this sauce very often. Usually she just uses the kind you buy in jars. But for this special recipe — which her grandmother had given her — she simmers real tomatoes with lots of different spices.

When the dough was finished, we'd flattened it onto a pizza pan, poured the sauce over it, then scattered slices of mozzarella and spread ricotta cheese over the whole thing.

The final touch was dotting it with pepperoni

slices. Mom had bought the cheese and pepperoni at a great gourmet store in downtown Stoneybrook. (That's the town in Connecticut where we live.)

Now the pizza lay on the kitchen table, a glistening work of art just waiting to be baked. I couldn't bear to think of this masterpiece being ruined by anchovies.

"Stacey?" Mom said. "Is one-third anchovies okay with you?"

"I don't know. What if they swim over to the rest of the pizza?" I asked.

"They're dead, Stacey," Mom reminded me, a smile forming on her lips.

"Oh, I know. It's just all so revolting, though. Last weekend when I visited Dad he told me those cherrystone clams on the half shell you guys like are still alive."

"You didn't know that?" Claudia asked, as if this were common knowledge. "Really? You didn't know?"

I shook my head. Maybe everyone else in the world had been informed that raw clams are still alive when you pop them in your mouth, but somehow I'd missed this fact. I found it nearly as disgusting as anchovies.

A fond, faraway look came into Mom's eyes. "Your dad and I used to travel all the way to Sheepshead Bay in Brooklyn to eat clams by the marina there," she told us.

I assumed she was talking about a time when they *both* lived in New York City. Back when they used to be married to each other.

"That was before you were born," she added. She smiled at me. "It's hard to believe fifteen years have passed since that time."

"That's more than my whole life," Claudia put in. (She and I are thirteen.)

"I know," Mom said. "In fact, I remember thinking I had food poisoning because I felt so sick one night after having clams at the marina. The next day I went to the doctor and discovered I was pregnant with Stacey. After she was born we somehow never went back to Sheepshead Bay again. Life just became so busy."

"Well, I feel sick when I even *look* at those anchovies," I said. "But I suppose if I just close my eyes . . . Okay, I guess. You can put them on."

"Never mind," Mom said. "I don't want them to ruin your appetite."

"No, really, you can have them," I insisted, feeling bad for making such a fuss. I hadn't wanted to be selfish. After all, Mom had done most of the pizza making. "I'll be fine," I added.

Once the horrible wormlike fishies were on the pie, Mom slid it into the preheated oven.

"It's Scrabble time!" she announced. But one look at Claudia's pained expression stopped her. "What's the matter?" she asked. "I thought we agreed to play a board game for Girls' Night at Home. Don't you like Scrabble?"

I knew exactly why Claudia didn't want to play Scrabble. In order to play Scrabble you have to be able to spell, and Claudia can't spell to save her life. It seemed rude to blurt that out, though.

Lately, I was pretty sensitive about what I said and did around Claudia. She and I had only recently worked things out after a huge fight. Even though we'd been best friends for a long time, our argument had been so big that at one point I doubted we'd ever be friends again.

The fight was over a boy. Both of us had liked him, but he liked me. At first. Then he started to like Claudia.

What a mess!

Neither of us was involved with him anymore.

Thank goodness our fight was over. Still, I didn't want to say anything to make Claudia mad again. I wasn't sure we were as close as we'd once been. The fight had left us on shaky ground. I was glad she was staying over tonight. It felt like old times.

"How about Monopoly?" I suggested.

"You just want to play that because you're so good at math," Mom objected.

That was true. Math *is* my best subject and it's helpful when playing Monopoly. Here's a weird thing: People sometimes tell me that I don't look like someone who would be good at math. For some reason, if you're pretty, with blue eyes and blonde hair (like me), some people think you're dumb. (I'm not being conceited; people do say I'm pretty.) To be honest, I don't see what looks have to do with who you are as a person — on the inside, I mean. But it seems important to a lot of people.

Anyway, Mom had a point. She knew I could clobber her at Monopoly. I always did.

"What about Sorry, then?" I suggested.

"Sorry is good," Claudia agreed.

"Then Sorry it is," Mom said. She left the room to find the game and returned with it quickly. We set up at the kitchen table.

During the game, Mom kept drifting off, not paying attention. We continually had to remind her it was her turn. Then she'd look startled and pick up her card. She didn't make all the best moves either. Somehow, her mind wasn't there. I wondered if she was still thinking about those evenings at Sheepshead Bay, eating clams with my father.

The oven had made the room hot and Mom opened the window over the sink. A warm spring breeze blew in and ruffled her hair. I could almost picture her sitting on the outdoor porch of a Brooklyn restaurant eating clams with Dad, a soft wind from the bay ruffling her hair in the same way.

My parents have been divorced for awhile now. The marriage hadn't been horrible. At least it never seemed that way to me (and I was there for most of it). The terrible fights had happened only toward the end. We didn't often discuss how Mom felt about it now.

The oven timer buzzed and the three of us jumped up. With her mitts on, Mom opened the oven door. The cheese bubbled as she slid the pizza out.

"Ohhh, yummmmm," Claudia said, breathing in.

"Something wonderful I can actually eat," I commented. Lots of other treats are off-limits to me because they're too sugary. I have a medical condition called diabetes. My body can't properly regulate the amount of sugar in my blood. To deal with it and stay healthy, I need to give myself injections of insulin each day. I also have to eat a very controlled diet, which means not letting myself get hungry and carefully balancing what I eat.

"Oh, gosh. Stacey, I suddenly have a headache," Mom said as she laid the pan on the stovetop. Frowning, she rubbed her forehead.

"Can I get you some aspirin or something?" I asked.

"Thanks, sweetie. I'll get some from the upstairs medicine cabinet." She pressed her palm to her forehead. "If you girls don't mind, I'll take my anchovy-covered slices and eat them in my room."

"We don't mind," I replied, handing her a plate.

She cut herself a large slice. Then, with a forced smile, she left.

"I hope she's okay," Claudia said, her eyes still on the kitchen door my mother had just gone through.

"Me too," I agreed as I cut slices for Claud and me. "Did she seem a little weird to you tonight?" I asked.

Claud nodded.

"I thought so too. Maybe it's because she was talking about my dad."

"Does she miss him?" Claudia wondered.

"I don't think so," I replied. She'd never said she

wanted to patch things up between them. She also knew he had a serious relationship with a woman named Samantha. "Maybe she just had a bad day at work."

Mom is a buyer at Bellair's department store in downtown Stoneybrook. Being a buyer means she's one of the people who selects the products Bellair's will sell to its customers. She likes her job but sometimes it's pretty hectic.

"Maybe," said Claud. "But she didn't mention her job once."

"I know. If it isn't work, though, and it isn't Dad, what else could it be?"

Chapter 2

I was still worrying about my mom the next day as I rode the train from Stoneybrook down to New York City. I do this regularly, since I often spend Saturdays and Sundays with Dad, who lives there. I love Manhattan, probably because I'm a city kid at heart. I was born in the Big Apple and lived there until a few years ago when we moved to Stoneybrook.

Last night, Mom had finally come out of her room saying her headache was better. Claudia and I were watching a video and she joined us for about fifteen minutes of it. Then she excused herself at the moment in the movie when the couple was fighting. Had the movie reminded her of the fights she and my father used to have?

This morning she still seemed . . . *off*. Faraway,

as if something were on her mind. In fact, she forgot to set her alarm — something she never does. I hadn't set mine, figuring that she would wake me up as usual. As a result, we were both running around, rushing to get to the station on time for my train.

"Have fun in the city," Claudia said that morning as she traipsed, still sleepy-eyed, to the front door, dragging her overnight bag behind her.

"Thanks. I'll see you Sunday," I told her, hopping on one foot as I tried to pull on my shoe.

After Claudia left, I wanted to talk to Mom, but she was rushing around so fast I couldn't find a moment. And in the car she was so intent on her driving, trying to make time, that then didn't seem like the right moment to talk either.

So there I was on the train, still thinking about Mom, not having a clue as to what was bothering her. As I gazed out the window, the train pulled into a tunnel. The tunnel was a familiar landmark on the train ride. It meant I was approaching Grand Central Station in New York.

I rummaged around in my backpack and found a brush. I swept it through my hair. Then I looked at my reflection in the window and applied a light coat of tinted lip gloss and brushed my cheeks with a dash of iridescent face glitter. (I wasn't sneaking. Mom allows me to wear makeup. I just hadn't had time to put it on at home.)

For the final touch, I slipped on two gold hoop earrings, which I'd stuck in my pocket as I'd hurried out of my bedroom. I don't usually go through so much preparation to meet Dad, but today he wouldn't be the first person I'd see.

I was meeting Ethan before Dad came.

The darkness of the tunnel gave way to the harsh lights of the station. Looking out the window, I spotted Ethan right away. He was leaning against one of the blue metal girders on the station platform, waiting for me.

With a hiss of brakes, the train stopped. I gathered my bags and was one of the first people off the train. "Ethan!" I called to him, waving my free arm.

He turned his head toward my voice. When he saw me, his face lit up.

What a face. Every time I see it, it's like the first time I saw him. I'm amazed all over again by his wide smile, his high cheekbones, his expressive eyes.

When I'd met him he'd had long brown hair, but recently he cut it short. I was finally used to the new short-haired Ethan and I had to admit the cut made his face shine.

I sound like I'm in love with him, don't I? Well, I am. And I'm not. What I mean is, I'm not sure. (I'm only thirteen.)

Ethan and I used to be a couple. But keeping up a relationship when one of us lived in Manhattan and the other in Stoneybrook became awfully difficult. So we broke up.

Then we worked on being friends. And now we were such good friends that those other "more than friends" feelings were coming back.

They were coming back to me, anyway. And I was pretty sure from some things Ethan had said lately — little hints — that they were returning to him too.

He took my overnight bag and we walked along the platform with the other passengers from the train. "We don't have a ton of time," he told me, checking his watch. "I have an art class in an hour."

Ethan is a serious art student. He's fifteen and attends an art high school in the city. He also takes extra classes at the Artists' Studio, an art school.

"That's perfect," I said. "Dad's meeting me by the information booth in an hour. We can eat here in the station." There are lots of shops with all kinds of foods in Grand Central.

"Okay," he agreed. So we stepped into a bakery.

He bought a sticky cinnamon bun and I chose a plain muffin. When we meet like this, we call it "having coffee." The funny part is, both of us hate coffee. He ordered a hot chocolate and I had tea.

We carried our things down the wide stairs to the dining area on the lower level. High-backed benches are set up there. They look like the pews in a church. We settled into one of them.

"How are things going with Claudia?" he asked, taking a bite of his bun.

"Better," I told him. "She stayed over last night."

"So things are back to normal?"

"Not exactly. There's still a little . . . you know . . . tension. But I think things will smooth out. My mother's the one I'm worried about."

"Really? How come?"

I explained what was going on, and Ethan asked if she'd been to the doctor lately. That worried me until I thought about it and realized she hadn't.

We were still talking about Mom when I spotted my dad coming down the stairs. I called to him.

"I was a little early," he said, "so I thought I'd come down to see what they've done here. I haven't been to the lower level since they renovated it."

"It's nice, isn't it?" I said.

"Very," he agreed, looking around. His eyes rested on Ethan.

"I came in early so we could visit," I explained.

"Hi, Mr. McGill," Ethan said.

"Hello, Ethan. How's the art world these days?"

"Fine, I guess. I'm kind of busy finishing up end-of-semester projects." He glanced at a wall clock. "In fact, I'd better go or I'll be late for the Saturday class. 'Bye, Stace. Call me."

"Or I'll e-mail you," I agreed, waving.

He hurried toward the stairs and Dad turned to me. "So . . . are you and Ethan . . . ?"

"We're just friends. We live too far away to be anything else."

"Maybe that's the best thing for now," Dad said.

That made me smile. It was so *Dad*. When Ethan and I were dating, he was always worried that we were spending too much time together or getting too serious. I was sure "just friends" was the way Dad liked my relationship with Ethan.

It was nothing personal against Ethan. Dad likes him. It's just that Ethan is a boy.

"Hungry?" Dad asked.

"I just ate."

He clapped his hands together and smiled.

"Okay, then. Why don't we head back to the apartment. Samantha's coming over later and we thought the three of us would go to the park. It's turning into a gorgeous day."

"Sounds good." Samantha Young, Dad's girlfriend, is really nice. It would be fun to go to the park with them.

He whistled a show tune as we walked up the stairs and headed across the main floor. "Why are you so happy?" I asked.

"What are you saying?" he asked. "That I'm usually an old grouch?"

I laughed. "No. You just seem especially happy, that's all."

"Why shouldn't I be? It's the weekend. My fabulous daughter is with me. I'm going to spend a great day with my two best girls."

My two best girls.

Of course, he meant Samantha and me. I remembered, though, a time when he'd called Mom and me his two best girls. It seemed a little weird now for him to be referring to *Samantha* and me in the same way. But I shrugged off the uncomfortable feeling.

We took a cab uptown to Dad's apartment. After the divorce, he'd found a two-bedroom place so that

I'd have my own room. I like it there. It's sort of my second home.

Samantha wasn't due to arrive until two, so I decided to get my homework out of the way. I stretched out on my bed with my science book and notebook to answer the questions we'd been assigned.

I'd left my door open. It faces out into the living room and I could see Dad seated behind his desk going over paperwork. He's the vice-president of a big company and he's devoted to his work.

It had been a serious problem between my mother and him. She began to resent the amount of time he spent at his office. Dad's being away so much didn't bother me at the time. It was just the way it had always been. Sure, I minded when he couldn't go on vacations with us, but, well, that was just Dad.

The funny thing is that now that I no longer live with Dad full-time, I see more of him than ever. He makes special time for me. He rarely did that when he and Mom were married and I was always around.

I could have minded that lately he was bringing Samantha along on things we did during our time together, but I didn't. She has a good sense of humor and she's generally more adventuresome than Dad.

For example, she was the one who talked him into going to Times Square to watch the ball drop last New Year's Eve. Dad wanted to watch it at home on TV.

With Samantha around, we do fun things. I guess you could say she's a lively person. Plus, she's always doing thoughtful things for Dad and me. When she comes over, she often brings some interesting thing she's bought. Dad seems very happy with her.

At about 1:45, Samantha arrived. (She has her own set of keys.) Her shoulder-length brown hair was pulled back into a bun. A pair of Rollerblades was slung over her shoulder. "Ready to roll?" she asked.

"I am!" I cried, jumping up from my bed. I keep my Rollerblades at the apartment because I Rollerblade more when I'm here than in Stoneybrook. I flung open my closet and began to dig for them.

"Do I have to skate too?" Dad asked, groaning.

Samantha sat on the couch. "Not if you don't want to, but don't expect us to wait for you."

My Rollerblades were way in the back of the closet. As I pulled them free, I heard Dad and Samantha talking softly in the living room. Why were they being so quiet, as if they didn't want me to hear what they were saying? I strained to listen, but I couldn't make out their words.

"I'm ready!" I called, heading out of my room. Dad took the blades Samantha had given him for his birthday from a box under the couch, and we headed for Central Park.

We had a great time, skating along the park paths, though it might have been better if we hadn't had to keep slowing down for Dad to catch up. He's not too swift on his wheels yet.

Dad said we were going to go out to dinner later, so we just bought a snack from a vendor. I love the potato knishes they sell. Dad and Samantha ate hot dogs with sauerkraut while the three of us sat together on a bench beside a path.

Dad suddenly turned to Samantha. "I hope you don't mind, but I just can't wait until dinner tonight to tell Stacey," he said.

Samantha smiled at him. "All right. Tell her now."

"Tell me what?" I asked.

Part of me already knew what he was going to say.

Chapter 3

I waited, just in case I was wrong.

"Samantha and I are getting married," Dad announced.

"I knew it!" I cried.

"You did?" said Samantha.

"I did! Somehow I just had a feeling."

"You look happy about it. Are you?" Dad asked.

"Totally! It's great."

Dad and Samantha looked relieved. Had they thought I'd be upset?

Why should I be? Samantha is a terrific person. And I knew my parents weren't going to get back together. Neither of them had made even a single move in that direction.

No, this was good. Dad was always happy when he was with Samantha — so I was all for it.

"When?" I asked.

"I'd like a really big wedding," Samantha replied. "Doing it whole hog takes at least a year to plan."

"A year!" I exclaimed. "Why so long?"

"The place for the reception has to be reserved, and the band, and the caterer," Samantha explained. "Those things are usually booked at least a year ahead. That's if you're fussy about getting exactly what you want."

"And believe me, she's fussy," Dad put in, teasing.

Samantha smiled at him. "That's why I'm marrying you. I never settle for second best."

"Where will you live?" I asked.

"In Ed's apartment," Samantha answered. "Don't worry. Your room will stay just as it is."

"I wasn't worried about that," I said, which was true. In fact, I wasn't worried about anything. I was thrilled that Samantha was going to become a permanent part of my life.

Around five we returned to Dad's apartment to clean up for dinner. We'd meet Samantha again at her place at six.

I stood in the shower, letting the warm water soothe my muscles, which ached just a little from all the Rollerblading. It occurred to me that I'd soon have a stepparent.

I thought about friends of mine who had stepparents.

My friend Kristy Thomas hadn't been crazy about her stepfather, Watson, at first. I didn't understand it. Watson always seemed like a good guy to me. Maybe it was because Watson brought big changes into her life.

Kristy and her brothers had moved across town to Watson's mansion. (He's a millionaire!) And Watson had kids from his former marriage, Karen and Andrew. Kristy had had to adjust to them, as well as to Watson.

Samantha didn't have kids to meet or a mansion to live in. I wouldn't have to move — not even out of my room. I wouldn't have all the changes Kristy had had. Besides, even with the rocky start, Kristy now loves Watson, and her family life is happy. It just took some getting used to.

Then there's my friend Mary Anne Spier. You might have thought she'd be thrilled to have a stepmother, since her own mother had died when Mary Anne was just a baby.

She wasn't, though.

In the beginning, she and Sharon, her stepmother,

clashed about lots of things — such as Mary Anne's cat, Tigger (Sharon didn't like him), and even about what to eat for dinner. (Sharon's a vegetarian; Mary Anne and her father aren't.)

Like Kristy, Mary Anne had to move to a new house. She and her father went to Sharon's. She also had to learn to live with a stepsister, Sharon's daughter, Dawn. That should have been a cinch since she and Dawn had been friends before their parents married (they'd even plotted to get them together in the first place), but it wasn't easy. Still — as with Kristy — everything smoothed out. Sharon and Mary Anne are now super-close.

All in all, I was pretty sure everything would be fine.

That night, we went to Windows on the World, a restaurant on top of one of the towers of the World Trade Center. The city lights shone like jewels below us. From up there you can see all the way to Brooklyn and Queens and across the Hudson River to New Jersey. I saw the torch of the Statue of Liberty glowing over the dark water.

Since we'd come to such a special restaurant, I knew Dad considered this a celebration. "When did you guys decide to get engaged?" I asked as the headwaiter led us to our table.

"Your dad proposed just last night," Samantha said, her smile beaming. She looked gorgeous in a violet sheath dress, her hair curling loosely around her shoulders.

"Am I the first to know?" I asked.

"Absolutely," Dad replied. "But now that we have your blessing, we can tell the world."

Samantha took hold of my hand. "I am so looking forward to really getting to know you," she said.

Getting to know me? What was she talking about? We already knew each other, didn't we?

"I mean, getting to know each other *better*," she clarified.

"Me too," I answered.

Dinner was wonderful, but Samantha's words stayed in the back of my mind. Did I really know Samantha? Sure, she was nice and fun. She loved Dad. But that was all I could say about her right now.

I found myself watching her during dinner, trying to observe things about her I hadn't noticed before. For the very first time I observed that she didn't drink anything while she ate. Not that it meant anything, but were there other things about her I hadn't noticed?

For the rest of the evening I studied her, but I

didn't notice anything else, except that she sometimes fiddled with the charms on her gold charm bracelet. Did those charms have particular meaning for her? Did they mark special events in her life? If so, what were they? I had no idea.

We took a cab to Dad's building, where he and I got out first while Samantha continued home. "Isn't she great?" Dad said, watching the cab turn the corner.

"She is," I agreed. "Where is she from?"

"Philadelphia. Why?"

I shrugged. "Just wondering." There was so much I didn't know.

That night I lay in bed having crazy thoughts. What if Dad was marrying a secret agent, a witch, an alien?

Not long ago I saw a late-night movie on TV about a woman who thought she was marrying a wonderful guy — a great stepfather to her kids — but he turned out to be a homicidal maniac!

Finally, I told myself I was being silly, rolled over, and fell asleep.

Around eleven the next morning, Dad woke me. "Hey, sleepyhead! Get dressed. We're going to meet Samantha for brunch at twelve."

"Where?" I asked groggily.

"The Oyster Bar at Grand Central. That way we won't have to worry about you missing your train, since we'll be there already."

"Cool," I said, climbing out of bed. Dad was still in a great mood. I love the Oyster Bar, but it's expensive. We don't go there all that often. I was glad that Dad felt like celebrating again.

I didn't want to miss my train either. I was going to a party that evening. More of a get-together, really. It was a welcome-home for my friend Mallory Pike. She was returning from her boarding school in Massachusetts, which had already let out for summer vacation. I was excited about seeing her again and I didn't want to be late for the party.

When we arrived at the restaurant, Samantha was already there, waiting in front. Once again, she looked amazing, this time in a lightweight, cream-colored suit. Her hair was gathered in a loose bun.

She and Dad kissed, and we went inside. The place was bustling. On one side people sat lined up along three counters.

On the other, where we were seated, the tables were close together, covered in plain white paper. Around us, people were eating clam chowder, shrimp, and all sorts of seafood.

Arched, tiled ceilings seemed to pick up every sound — every voice, every clattering dish — and echo it around the cavernous space. It's not especially fancy, but there's something so . . . New York . . . about the Oyster Bar, and the food is great.

After we ordered, Dad excused himself to go to the rest room. "I was thinking about you last night," Samantha said to me when he was gone. "Soon we'll be spending more time together than ever. I hope you're all right about that."

"I'm fine about it," I assured her.

"I need to say this right away," she continued. "I don't expect you to think of me as another mother. Please don't worry about that. You already have a wonderful mother and I don't want to compete with her in any way."

I nodded. It was nice of her to say that about my mother.

"I hope we can simply go on developing the terrific relationship we've already started," she said.

"That sounds good to me," I said, feeling a little silly for having worried about Samantha the night before. She was wonderful! I'd get to know more about her a little bit at a time. No problem.

Dad returned just as our waiter arrived with the

food. My order — a variety of smoked fishes — was delicious. We ate, talked, and laughed until ten minutes before my train was scheduled to depart.

Dad paid our bill, then he and Samantha walked with me to the platform. The train was already there, but the doors were still shut. While we waited for them to open, an unsettling thought occurred to me.

"When are you going to tell Mom?" I asked Dad.

Dad took a long breath. "I suppose I should call her soon. Or maybe she should hear it from you, Stacey."

I shook my head. "I don't think so."

"It's really your job, Ed," Samantha said gently.

"Okay, you're right."

A bell rang and the doors whooshed open. A loudspeaker announced that my train was now boarding.

I kissed Dad and Samantha, then stepped onto the train. As I settled into my seat, I wondered how I'd manage to keep this big news from Mom until Dad called her.

Chapter 4

Mom was standing on the platform when the train pulled into the Stoneybrook station. She smiled as I approached her. "Hi, honey!" she cried.

The distracted look was gone from her face. She was happy to see me. She hugged me, then pulled back, concerned. "What's wrong?"

"Nothing. Why?"

"When I hugged you, you felt tense. What's bothering you?" Her eyes searched my face for a clue.

I knew exactly what was bothering me, of course. Should I tell her the news?

No, I couldn't. Dad was the one who was supposed to do it.

"I had a nice weekend," I insisted. "I saw Ethan for a quick visit. Dad took us to two nice restaurants. It was great."

"He took you and Ethan?"

"Um, no. Samantha and me."

"Oh," said Mom in that flat voice she sometimes uses when the subject of my father comes up.

We walked silently to the car. Mom unlocked it and I tossed my overnight bag into the backseat.

"Is it Samantha?" Mom asked, sliding behind the wheel. "Is that what's bothering you? Because if it is, it's okay. I understand that your dad dates Samantha. I don't want you to feel disloyal to me if you spend time with her while you're there."

"Oh, I don't," I replied. "I mean, I know you're my mother. And Samantha is . . . Samantha."

Again, she seemed to search my face. "But something else *is* bothering you," she said finally.

I sighed. There was no sense holding back. She'd get it out of me sooner or later. "Sort of," I told her.

"What?"

"Dad and Samantha are getting married."

Mom froze, her hand still on the key.

I felt terrible — as if I'd taken a bat and hit her with it. If I could have snatched my words out of the air and pulled them back, I would have.

It was too late for that, though. I'd delivered the news, and now we'd have to deal with her reaction.

She took her hand off the key and slowly sat back in her seat, staring straight ahead.

My mind raced, searching for the right words to make her feel better. But I couldn't find them. What was there to say? That the marriage would make Dad unhappy, or that he wouldn't go through with it? That Samantha was horrible? But there was no sense telling lies. All I could do was sit there with her as she absorbed the information.

After another moment, she turned to me. Her expression was calm, though her brow was furrowed. "You like Samantha, don't you?" she asked.

I nodded.

Mom mirrored my nod. "Well, then, I guess that's that."

Turning the key in the ignition, she started the car and pulled out of the lot. We drove home in silence. She didn't seem to want to chat. Besides, everything I'd tell her about the weekend involved Dad and Samantha. So I kept my mouth shut. Mom would talk again when she was ready.

We pulled into our driveway. Mom went into the house without waiting for me. When I walked through the front door, the house was quiet and I didn't see her anywhere.

I put down my overnight bag and checked the

living room, then the kitchen. I couldn't imagine where she'd gone. I didn't know what to do, so I picked up my bag and went upstairs to unpack.

As I passed Mom's door, I heard her crying.

The last time I'd stood in the hallway and listened to her cry was when she and Dad were still married. The sound of her sobs brought everything back to me — the shouting, the slamming of doors, the cruel words.

But while I was thinking of the bad times, was she remembering the good ones? Was she wishing she and Dad were still together?

I knocked softly on her door. Her crying stopped abruptly. "Are you all right?" I asked.

She sniffed. "I'm okay. You can come in."

I found her sitting at the end of her bed, her eyes puffy.

She smiled sadly. "Sorry for acting this way. I don't know why I'm crying. Honestly." Tears came back to her eyes but she wiped them away. "I feel completely stupid."

I sat beside her on the bed. "You don't have to be sorry. I guess it's sort of a shock."

"He should have told me himself," she said, a hint of anger in her voice.

"He's going to. He said he'll call . . . tonight, I think."

She nodded. "Then I suppose this is a new development."

"Brand-new."

She stood up and took a tissue from the box on her dresser. Wiping her eyes, she straightened her shoulders. "It's not as though I thought we were ever getting back together. I didn't. Maybe I'm crying because I don't know what else to do. Or because something in my life is ending. Endings are always hard for me to deal with, even if they're for the best. As she spoke, she calmed down. "Stacey, I'm not going to wait for your father's phone call. Would you stay with me while I call him?"

"All right," I agreed. I'd have expected her to want privacy, but maybe she couldn't stand to be alone while she did this. I sat there on the bed as she punched Dad's number in on her cordless phone.

"Oh, hello," Mom said after a moment. She blinked hard and I had the distinct feeling Samantha had answered. "This is Maureen . . . Maureen McGill." She coughed.

Yes, it was definitely Samantha.

"That's nice to hear . . . she is a lovely girl . . .

thank you. She told me your exciting news. Congratulations."

Good for you, Mom! I cheered silently. I was proud of her for being so classy.

"You're welcome. Is Ed there?" she continued. "Thank you."

I crossed my fingers as she waited for Dad to come to the phone. She had turned her back to me, but I could still see her face in the mirror over her dresser. She'd shut her eyes as if gathering her strength for the conversation with my dad.

"Ed," she said, opening her eyes again. "Stacey told me your news. . . . Yes, she mentioned that you planned to call, but I didn't want to wait. When's the big day? . . . Oh, I see. Well, these things take time. I just wanted to congratulate you. . . . Of course. We'll speak again soon, I'm sure. Bye-bye."

In the mirror I saw her put her hand over her heart. It must have been pounding. She shut her eyes again and just stood there.

I slid off the bed and stood beside her, also facing the mirror, and rested my head on her shoulder.

Two tears ran down her cheeks but she brushed them away and opened her eyes. Turning, she kissed the top of my head lightly.

To my surprise, tears leaped to my eyes. What

was *I* crying about? I really didn't know. Maybe it was just seeing my mother so sad and admiring her bravery in calling Dad.

Mom noticed my tears. "Are you all right about this?" she asked, looking into my eyes. "Their marriage?"

I nodded. "It doesn't really change anything," I said in a choked voice.

"You're right," she agreed, her eyes welling once again. "So why are we crying?"

"I have no idea. But I'm very proud of you."

"The same here," Mom said. Then we both cried a little harder and held each other very tight.

Chapter 5

I stood toweling my hair dry after my shower and staring into my closet. I was trying to decide what to wear to Mallory's welcome-home party. But all I could think about was Mom and how upset she'd been. I pulled flared-leg khakis from a hanger and held them up for inspection. Instead of checking them out, though, I pictured Mom's tearstained face.

"Oh, forget it," I mumbled, tossing the pants onto the bed. I couldn't leave Mom now. Mallory would just have to understand.

I stepped into the hall and heard Mom moving around downstairs. I followed the sounds to the kitchen, where Mom was unloading the dishwasher.

"How about a game of Monopoly?" I proposed, hoping she'd laugh at the suggestion.

She didn't, though. Instead, she said, "Don't you have a party to go to soon?"

I flopped into a kitchen chair. "I don't feel like going."

"Since when? You were looking forward to it. On Friday you made a big deal about catching an early train today so you'd be home in time."

I shrugged. "It doesn't matter."

"You're staying home to be with me, aren't you?"

"I don't mind."

But I did mind, kind of.

I was dying to see Mallory. Her parents were driving down from Massachusetts with her today. And all my friends would be at her house, waiting for her. I really wanted to see her face when she walked in the door and we surprised her.

Still, this was more important.

"You're very sweet, honey. I really appreciate it, but I'm fine," Mom insisted. "There's absolutely no need for you to stay. Honestly."

"I'm staying, Mom." I tried to sound firm.

"Stacey, if you stay home because of me — I'll go out."

"What?"

"Yes. In fact, that's exactly what I'll do. I mean,

what I'll do anyway. I'll call Beverly and see if she wants to go to a movie. Maybe I'll call a bunch of other people from work too. We'll make a group evening out of it," she said, taking the receiver from the wall phone.

"Okay." I gave in, standing up. "If you're sure."

"I'm positive," she said as she punched in her friend's number. "Now go get dressed."

As I went back upstairs, I wasn't sure if she was really feeling better, or if she was just putting on a brave front for me. Either way, going out with her friends from work was probably the best thing she could do tonight. It would take her mind off Dad, and she always seems to have fun with her work friends anyway.

In my room, I slipped into the khakis, pulled on a short-sleeved ribbed tee with a wide stripe running across the top, and slid on my platform slides.

I brushed my hair back off my face and held it in place with small butterfly clips.

"Ready?" Mom called from her room.

"Almost," I called back.

On tiptoe, I reached up to my closet shelf and pulled down a gift bag. The weekend before last, when I'd been in the city, I had gone to a cool makeup and accessories place on Columbus Avenue. I'd bought Mallory a welcome-home gift.

It was an assortment of fun things — fancy hair clips, a macramé hemp choker, a packet of small pale-colored lip glosses, some colorful rubber bangle bracelets, stuff like that.

When I ran out into the hall, Mom was waiting, looking very spiffy, and almost happy. "Let's go," she said with a smile.

Outside, the air was warm, definitely springlike. Although it was six-thirty, the sun was still up. That's one of the things I love most about spring and summer, the long days.

I cut through my backyard to the Pikes' backyard. I hadn't been to their house since my last baby-sitting job for the Pike family. I should say my last *co*-baby-sitting job: There are so many Pike kids — seven plus Mallory! — that the BSC always sends two sitters.

There's Mallory, who is eleven. She's not actually there most of the time, since, as I said, she goes to boarding school. And she doesn't need a sitter. Before she left, she was an important part of the BSC herself. After her come the ten-year-old triplets, Byron, Jordan, and Adam. Next is Vanessa, who is nine.

Then comes Nicky, who's eight, Margo, who's seven, and finally Claire, who's five.

It's a wild household, and it was at its wildest that evening. I knocked on the door and rang the bell for almost a minute before Mary Anne opened it.

"Sorry you had to wait," said Mary Anne. "It's so noisy in here I didn't hear you until just now. Were you there long?"

"Not too long," I replied, shouting to be heard. The triplets were chasing after Nicky and Vanessa, who were throwing something back and forth between them. All of them were shouting.

Claire wailed loudly as my friend Jessi Ramsey rubbed her elbow and tried to comfort her. Claire stopped crying when she saw me. "I fell," she explained with a sniff.

Jessi smiled at me and smoothed her hand over her black hair, which she wore pulled back in a bun. "It's been nuts here," she reported. "This party needed more planning. We're kind of throwing it together now."

"Throwing is not the word!" Another friend, Abby Stevenson, came in from the kitchen holding a bunch of multicolored balloons. (Abby used to be a BSC member too but dropped out because her schedule was so busy with other things, especially sports.)

She rolled her eyes. "This party is being tossed together in a storm of confusion. If I have to blow up another one of these balloons I'll pass out."

Claudia and Margo walked in from the kitchen, their arms piled high with cans of soda. Whatever it was that Nicky was throwing to Vanessa sailed over Adam's head and hit Margo. She jumped back, knocking Claudia off balance. Both of them dropped their cans, which rolled and spun around the living room. One can opened slightly and began spewing soda in a foamy circle.

Margo screamed.

A piercing whistle came from the stairs.

The sound made me cringe and cover my ears. Looking up, I saw Kristy with two fingers between her lips.

Instantly, the room became quiet. The only sound was the fizz of the slowly spinning can as the last of the cola seeped out.

"Everybody chill!" Kristy commanded. She turned toward Nicky. "What are you guys throwing around?"

"Nothing!" Jordan said quickly. We all looked at Margo's feet, where a crumpled white cloth was lying.

Pow, the Pikes' basset hound, trotted to the cloth,

which was now soaked with cola, and brought it to Nicky.

He held the dripping cloth up for all to see. "Just a pair of Jordan's underpants. We were going to hang them outside for a welcome-home flag. But now they're kind of ruined."

Jordan grabbed them from him. "Jerk," he grumbled.

Kristy shook her head and rolled her eyes. "Mallory should be here any minute," she said. "And we're not even halfway ready."

She began organizing us. (Kristy is the president of the BSC and a natural leader.) She assigned Adam to make microwave popcorn, Jordan to clean the spilled soda, and Byron to pick up the soda cans and set them out neatly on the coffee table. Vanessa was put in charge of opening pretzel and potato chip bags. Margo was to bring out napkins and paper plates. And Claudia was in charge of supervising them.

Kristy told Jessi and Claire to pick out some tapes and CDs.

"Mary Anne, you put out the cake," she added.

"I'm here now too!" I reminded her.

"Oh, hi, Stacey," she said, as if she had just noticed me. She gazed around for something I could do. Her eyes lit on a long scroll of paper draped across the sofa. "Could you hang that banner somewhere?"

"I'll try."

The banner read WELCOME HOME, MALLORY!!!!

I found tape in a drawer, pulled up a chair to stand on, and began taping up the sign under the archway leading into the dining room.

One end was up when I heard a car pull into the driveway.

"They're here! They're here!" Adam cried.

As quickly as I could, I dragged the chair to the other side of the arch and taped up the loose end of the banner. I was climbing off my chair when the front door opened.

Mallory stepped in.

"Welcome home!" we all shouted in one happy voice.

Mallory stepped back, wide-eyed and smiling. "Wow! Thanks, you guys!" she said.

Claire and Margo flung themselves upon her, wrapping her in a hug. The rest of her brothers and sisters were right on top of them.

"You're squishing me!" Mallory laughed. "One at a time."

Mr. and Mrs. Pike came in behind her and were

almost knocked backward by their children. "Whoa, let her breathe," Mr. Pike advised them cheerfully.

When her brothers and sisters had gotten their share of hugs, they peeled off one by one. Then it was our turn to swamp Mallory with hugs. By the time we were done, her glasses had slid down her nose and her curls were even more tousled than usual.

"I'm glad to see all of you too," she said. "I've missed everybody so much. Thank goodness for e-mail."

I stepped back and studied her. Had she changed? Yes, a little. Not her appearance so much as attitude. She seemed to stand straighter, more confidently.

"Are you hungry?" Mary Anne asked her. "We have a chocolate cake, and there are chips and popcorn and pretzels and soda."

Mallory scooped up a handful of potato chips. "Did Claudia donate these from her private storehouse?" she joked.

"If you must know, I did," Claudia told her. Claudia is a junk food fanatic. Her parents don't approve of the stuff, so she hides it in her room.

"You know Claudia is our resource for all party treats," I said.

Mallory grinned at us. "So what have you two been up to lately?"

Claudia and I looked at each other. "Fighting, mostly," Claudia admitted.

"Everything okay now?" Mal asked cautiously.

Again, I looked to Claudia, checking. She looked to me, also checking. We both nodded, then turned to Mallory. "Yup," I said.

"Definitely," Claudia agreed.

Jessi joined us, placing one hand on Mallory's shoulder. Mallory put her arm around Jessi's waist. Like Mallory, Jessi is eleven. Before Mallory left, she and Jessi had been best friends.

I wondered how this separation would affect their friendship. Personally, I had seen almost as little of Jessi as I had of Mallory, even though Jessi was still right here in Stoneybrook. Jessi is a talented and devoted ballet dancer, and lately she'd been taking more lessons than ever. She also used to be a BSC member, but she dropped out because she's so busy with her classes at the Stamford Ballet School. (Stamford is the closest city to Stoneybrook.)

"Jessi, on the way home Mom was telling me about all these neat summer programs the Stoneybrook Community Center is offering this year,"

Mallory said. "This year we're old enough to take the sailing lessons. There are some computer classes I want to check out too, and I thought maybe we could learn tennis together."

Jessi shook her head. "Can't," she said. "I'm really sorry, but I have a full load of dance classes lined up already. The summer program at the ballet school is almost like summer school."

"Oh," Mallory said, sounding incredibly disappointed.

"Hey, Mallory," Claire called.

She stood under the welcome-home banner and held up a big piece of paper with letters scrawled on it in her childish handwriting. "I did this," she said proudly.

The paper read WE LOVE YOU, MALLORY.

"Your writing has improved so much," Mallory said, taking the paper.

"Byron helped me," Claire said, beaming at him.

"Byron?" Mallory repeated.

Claire nodded energetically. "He's the oldest now. He helps all of us."

"He's not older than me!" Adam chimed in, offended.

"Or me," Jordan objected.

"You're all the oldest," Claire agreed diplomatically. Then in a whisper she added, "But Byron is the nicest."

"*I'm* the oldest," Mallory protested. She tried to keep her voice light, but something told me she didn't like the idea of losing her number one spot in the family order.

"Not when you're not here you're not," Adam argued.

"Even then," Mallory insisted. As she spoke, the end of the banner I hadn't fastened securely came undone, and the banner fluttered down on top of her head. "I'm still the oldest," she said in a muffled voice from beneath the paper.

Chapter 6

"Here's the thing that's so weird," Claudia said the next day as we entered my kitchen through the side door.

"I'm actually considering still going out with Alan Gray." She tossed her backpack on a chair. We'd decided to study together for our science final. Claud sat in the chair beside her pack. "I mean, what do we always say after the name Alan Gray?"

"Ewwwwww! Yuck!" I supplied as I pulled open the refrigerator door.

"Exactly!" she agreed. "Eeeeewwww! Yuck! Why should I want to keep going out with someone like him?"

"Because he's changed?" I suggested. "He *has* shown a more serious side of himself lately."

Alan Gray was basically the class clown. But in the past he'd often gone too far, and my friends and I had thought of him as the class jerk. Lately, though, he and Claudia had been trying out the idea of dating each other.

"I suppose," Claudia agreed. "I keep thinking about the video interview you did with him for your project — how he complained that no one ever saw the real Alan. It got to me. But I don't know. What would kids think of me if I dated him seriously?"

"That you have a good sense of humor?" I suggested.

That made her laugh. "Maybe."

I bit into an apple and tossed one to Claudia. I know she would have preferred a Ring-Ding or something like that, but we just don't have that kind of food in the house. She bit into it anyway.

"I can't talk to my mother about it," she complained. "She's so old-fashioned. She'd say I shouldn't be so worried about boys. And Janine is in her own genius world. She never cares what anyone else thinks."

Janine is Claudia's sixteen-year-old sister. She has a sky-high IQ. What Claudia had said about her was true. She'd just tell Claudia not to care — to date

Alan if she liked him — which, of course, is good advice. But for most people, it's hard not to care at all about what other people think.

"My mom's usually pretty good to talk to," I said. "Want to try her?"

"Is she home?"

"No. She'll be home around five, though. You can probably catch her before we go back to your house for the BSC meeting."

With our backpacks and apples, we headed out of the kitchen and through the dining room. We were at the stairs when I stopped short.

Mom was sitting on the living room couch. "Mom!"

"Stacey!" she cried. Clearly, she'd been zoning out. Each of us had startled the other.

"Why are you home so early?" I asked, walking into the living room with Claudia behind me. "Are you sick?"

"No," she answered. "I finished up everything I had to do for the day and I just didn't feel like being in my office."

Her expression and tone were serious, as if she had something important on her mind. I noticed she'd begun reading a novel, but it lay facedown on the couch beside her. It seemed she'd just been sitting there, thinking. She was so deep in thought that she hadn't even heard us come in. What was she thinking about? I wondered. Dad?

I hesitated. "I'm glad you're home, because Claudia wants to talk to you about something," I said finally.

Claudia stepped closer. "Oh, yeah. Here's the thing." She laid out her conflict over Alan.

"Well," said Mom, "Anne Bancroft married Mel Brooks."

"Who are they?" Claudia asked.

"Anne Bancroft is a very well-respected actress who usually does serious roles. She's very elegant. And Mel Brooks is a zany comedian. What does it say about Anne Bancroft that she married Mel Brooks?"

"That she has a good sense of humor?" I repeated.

Mom smiled. "I suppose so. It also shows that she's her own person, not too concerned about her image. I suppose some people wondered why she married Mel Brooks, but they seem to be happy. Their marriage is one of the most long-standing in show business."

"Please!" Claudia objected. "I'm not *marrying* Alan!"

"You never know," Mom said. She laughed, but I caught something sad in it. "You can't always predict who you're going to marry or how it will work out."

The phone rang. "Excuse me," Mom said as she stood up to answer it.

"Did that help at all?" I asked Claudia.

"Sort of," she said. "It gave me something to think about, anyway."

We headed back to the stairs. "Your mom's still feeling down, huh," Claudia observed once we were in my room.

"I guess so. I'd say it was Dad and Samantha, but it seemed as if there was something on her mind even before I went to New York. Remember?"

"Yeah. Last Friday your mom *did* have something on her mind," she recalled as she sat cross-legged on my bedroom floor. "Do you think she's lonely?"

"Could be." I stretched out on my bed.

"Would she be happier if she were dating?"

I remembered once when I had played matchmaker. I was sitting for two kids who lived with their divorced father. John, their dad, had seemed perfect for Mom. I introduced them and almost immediately

John asked Mom out. Now that I thought about it, Mom *had* seemed happier while they were dating.

At least at first.

Then, slowly, Mom began to see traits in John she didn't like. Nothing awful. She thought he was impatient with his kids, and she said he was self-centered. So she broke it off.

"Even if she would be happier dating, what can I do about it?" I asked. "The last time I found someone for her to date it didn't exactly work out."

"I remember," Claudia said. "Besides, where would we find someone for her?"

I stood up and dug my science textbook out of my pack. Claudia took out hers.

"I've got it!" she cried suddenly. "I know where we can find a man for your mother. A video dating service!"

"Huh?"

"Definitely," she continued, excited. "We'll ask for a bunch of tapes of possible dates, and *we'll* pick out the good ones. After all, this guy could be a potential stepfather for you, so we have to be careful."

"Mom would never go for that," I objected.

"She won't know. We'll do all the work. That way she doesn't have to be anxious about it. This is perfect!"

"You know, it might work. How would we get tapes from a video dating service, though?"

Claudia's enthusiastic expression faded. "I have no idea," she said. "But there must be a way."

Chapter 7

A week later, Claudia called me after school just as I was heading out for a sitting job. "I think I almost have them," she said.

"Have what?"

"The date tapes."

"Oh, my gosh! How did you do it?"

Before she could answer there was a click on the line. "That's my call waiting," she said hurriedly. "It might be them. I'll call you later." With another click, she was gone.

I couldn't believe she'd actually gotten the tapes. What kind of men would be on them? Would they all be geeks or would there actually be someone right for Mom?

I didn't have time to stand around thinking about

it. I was supposed to be at the Pikes' to baby-sit with Mallory in five minutes.

As I walked around the block, I realized that I'd barely seen Mallory since her party. I'd been so busy with school, baby-sitting, and studying for finals. Also, I'd become used to her being gone. It no longer occurred to me to include her in things. It would be nice to spend the afternoon together.

Mallory opened the door. "Hi. Everything's calm for the moment. Come on in."

It *was* unusually quiet for the Pike household. "Where is everybody?" I asked.

Mallory nodded toward the upstairs. "Get this," she said. "Byron now helps them all with their homework as soon as they come home."

"No way."

"Yes way. It seems he jumped right into my spot the moment I was gone."

"But you never made everyone do homework as soon as they got in."

"I know. Not only is he determined to be the big brother, he wants to be the biggest big brother of all time."

"And the others go for it?"

"In a major way. They love having a big, oldest brother. They're crazy about it."

"What about Jordan and Adam?" I asked.

"They couldn't care less. They're so busy with sports and their friends."

I laughed. "Funny. Byron has always been Nicky's and the girls' older brother, but now that they think of him as the oldest he has a whole new status."

"I don't think it's funny," Mallory grumbled as we headed into the kitchen. "*I'm* the oldest in this family."

"Does it matter?" I asked. As an only child, I had no idea.

"Yes, it matters! All my life I've been . . . I don't know . . . in charge here. Now it's like I'm nobody!"

"Oh, come on. You could never be nobody. They were all so excited when you came back. They almost crushed you with hugs."

"I know. But that was then. The thrill has definitely worn off."

I realized something. Like me, the Pike kids had grown used to Mallory's being gone. They now had their own way of doing things, which didn't include her.

"Don't worry," I said. "They'll get used to your being home again, and everything will change back to the way it was."

"I hope so. I can't wait until summer."

"What do you mean? Your vacation has already started."

"I'm waiting for the rest of you guys to be free. Right now, no one's around most of the day."

"You love to read," I said. "It must be nice to have free time for that."

"A person can only read for so long. I've read eight books just since I've been home. By the end of this week I'll have completed my entire summer reading requirement."

"There's TV," I suggested feebly.

"Obviously you haven't watched much daytime TV lately. I really couldn't care less how to redecorate my home. I have only a tiny interest in celebrity interviews. I can't stand those shows where people fight about who did what to whom. That leaves game shows and daytime soaps."

"What about those?" I asked.

She buried her head in her hands. "I have become so pathetic! I actually know what couples are divorcing and who has a split personality and an evil twin." She lifted her head. "On every single channel!"

I patted her shoulder. "It'll get better," I assured her. "You've only been home a week."

"A week," she wailed. "I knew half the kids at

Riverbend in a week. How could it possibly be easier to adjust to a new boarding school than it is to re-adjust to your own home?"

"I don't know. But I bet you're right. Once school is out around here it'll change."

As we spoke, Vanessa came into the kitchen. "Oh, hi," she said when she saw us. Her tone had a tinge of frostiness.

At the same time, Margo ran in and pulled up a chair at the table. "Hi," she said. "So, Mallory, what did you do today while we were at school?"

"Nothing in particular," Mallory replied. "How was school?"

"Cool. We had a spelling contest to see who would get to bring home Graybaby — he's our chinchilla — over the summer. Everybody wanted to. Mom told me I couldn't, but I forgot and raised my hand anyway."

"Oh, no." Mallory gasped. "You didn't win, did you?"

"No. I was first runner-up, though," Margo said proudly. "If for any reason Robert Amato can't keep Graybaby, I get to bring him home."

"You'd better hope Robert can keep him," Mallory warned her.

"You should hope she gets Graybaby," Vanessa

said, her head in the refrigerator. "At least he would be someone for you to hang out with this summer."

I wondered where *that* little dig had come from. Was Vanessa still angry at Mallory for going away? She had been mad at first, but I thought she was over it.

"I'll have my friends to hang out with, thank you very much," Mallory replied coolly.

"I wouldn't be so sure," Vanessa replied in an annoying singsong voice as she poured herself a glass of milk. "When you leave town you can't expect everyone to just wait around for you to come back."

"What's that supposed to mean?" Mallory asked her angrily.

"Whatever you think it means."

Mallory slapped the table. "She's been acting like that for the last week!"

"She's mad at you," Margo offered. "She says you can't just come back and expect everyone to drop dead over you. Those were her exact words."

Mallory's jaw dropped.

Margo jumped up from the table. "Got to go," she said, bounding out of the room after Vanessa.

"See!" Mallory said to me. Her face was red, as if she wanted to cry but wouldn't let herself. "It's like I'm a stranger in my own house."

"Margo was friendly," I pointed out.

"She didn't stay, though, did she? She wants to be with the others all the time. Look what she just did. She dropped her little bomb about Vanessa being angry and then ran out. That's not exactly friendly."

I felt bad for Mal. Guilty too. I hadn't been much of a friend this last week. From now on I would try to do better.

Chapter 8

Claudia was waiting at my locker when I arrived at school on Wednesday morning. Her face glowed with excitement. "I have a tape," she said.

A slow grin spread across my face. I hadn't really thought she could do it. "You're a genius! How did you manage to get it?"

"I found the name of a dating service in the phone book. Then I called and said that I was a college student doing a project on computer dating for my social sciences class."

"College?"

She nodded, smiling, obviously very proud of herself. "The receptionist couldn't see me over the phone, so she didn't know I'm only thirteen. I thought a college paper sounded more serious. I told her I needed to see a tape in order to write the report. It came in the mail yesterday afternoon but I didn't see it lying on the table until this morning."

"Awesome," I said, opening my locker. "We can watch it at my house this afternoon. Mom won't be home."

"That's good," Claudia replied. "Janine will be home at my house. And you know how she can be." I did. Claudia's older sister was the type to tell her parents, who might not approve.

On our way to homeroom, we decided to make the afternoon a party of sorts. We'd invite our friends. "I'll call Mallory at lunchtime," I said, remembering the promise I'd made myself.

That afternoon, Claudia, Mary Anne, and Kristy walked home with me. We'd invited Jessi, but she was rushing off to dance class after school and Abby had soccer practice. Mallory had agreed to meet us at my house.

We'd been there only minutes, putting snacks together, when she knocked on the kitchen door. "Okay, where are these fabulous guys for your mom?" she said as I let her in. "Let's have a look at them."

"We should set up a rating system," Kristy suggested.

“How about a star rating, like hotels and restaurants,” I said.

“Or thumbs-up, thumbs-down,” Mary Anne offered.

We carried our snacks into the living room and placed them on the coffee table. Then Claudia slipped the tape into the VCR.

In minutes we were settled in, watching. First, a pretty woman with a smooth speaking voice came on and explained how the dating service worked. You were supposed to look at the tape and decide whether you’d like to meet a particular man from the video. If you did, the dating service sent him *your* tape and he would agree or decline to meet you. It worked the other way around too. If a man saw your tape and wanted to meet you, you could then view his tape and make a decision.

The first man to appear had a pleasant face. He looked about Mom’s age. He said he was a dentist. He liked pets, swimming, and traveling.

I paused the tape. “He seems nice.”

“Are you kidding? He’s bald!” Kristy cried.

“No, he’s not.” His hair was thinning, but I wouldn’t call him bald.

“He will be in about a week,” Kristy insisted.

"That doesn't matter," said Mary Anne. "Bald men can be very nice. Watson is a little bald."

"I know," replied Kristy. "That's what I mean. When Mom married Watson he had thin hair. It wasn't too bad. But he got more bald by the day. He's practically one big bald spot now."

"Does your mother mind?" Claudia asked.

"She *says* she doesn't. She tells Watson it's cute. But Watson minds. I see him checking it out in the mirror. It's awful. I could never go out with a bald guy."

"That's because you're thirteen!" cried Mary Anne. "There aren't too many balding thirteen-year-olds around, unless they shave their heads."

"Ew. I wouldn't go out with one of those shaved-head guys either," Kristy said.

"Sports stars sometimes shave their heads," I reminded her.

"Maybe then," Kristy grudgingly agreed. "But I don't like it."

"I don't think grown women mind baldness that much," Claudia commented. "I think they just accept it."

"How could they?" Kristy looked revolted. "Besides, what's with all this swimming? Your mother would always be at a pool or *traveling* to the beach. The guy loves traveling, after all." Kristy gave him a thumbs-down.

"Wow, you're tough," Claudia commented. "I thought he was kind of nice. Besides, it might be good to date a dentist if you ever had tooth trouble."

"Forget it," Kristy scoffed. "You'd have a toothache and he'd be off traveling around, looking for a good beach."

I held up the clicker and unpaused the tape. "Let's try the next guy."

The man who appeared on the screen was mildly good-looking, with *lots* of thick brown hair. "Hello, my name is Alex," he said. "I'm an accountant. I'm a fan of skydiving, bungee jumping, and surfing. I like to dance, eat fine foods, and have a good time with that special woman."

I paused the tape. "He's lying," I said.

"Why do you say that?" Mary Anne asked.

"Listen to his voice," I replied. "He sounds super-dull but he claims he likes to do all this exciting stuff."

"That doesn't prove he's lying," Mary Anne objected.

"No, just that he's an idiot," Mallory put in.

"Why?" Mary Anne asked.

"Bungee jumping has to be the stupidest activity in the world," Mallory replied.

"Actually, I can't see my mom with a bungee jumper," I agreed.

"She'd like to eat fine food and dance, though," Mary Anne said. "He's kind of cute too."

"Yeah, and he could do her taxes for her," Kristy added. She shot her thumb up.

"Okay, it's a tie so far. Mary Anne and Kristy are thumbs-up. Mallory and I are thumbs-down." I turned to Claudia. "You're the tiebreaker."

She pointed her thumb down. "That voice of his would drive me nuts. He sounds like the cat Garfield, on TV."

I started the video again. The third man had a lined face, curly black-and-gray hair, and a nice smile. "I'm Roy," he said with the trace of some kind of accent. "I'm a stamp collector. That's not my job. It's a hobby. I haven't worked in awhile, which is not to say I'm a bum. I have a bad back and I collect disability from my union. Anyway, because of the back, sports are out, so don't expect to be Rollerblading or anything. But if you like the movies, theater, concerts, I'm your guy."

"He's the one," Mallory said. "If I were older, I'd go out with him."

"*Much* older," Claudia commented. "He could be Stacey's grandfather, not her stepfather."

"Yeah, and he'd never want to *do* anything because of his back," Kristy added. "Your mother likes to jog and bike ride."

"She could do that with her other friends. He seems like such a nice man," Mallory said. She looked at his face. "Wouldn't he be a cute stepfather, Stacey?"

"I don't know. He'd be nice to have as an uncle or a neighbor. I couldn't see my mother dating him."

"He sort of bottoms out on the attractiveness scale too," Claudia said.

"Not as dreamy as Alan Gray, huh?" Kristy teased her.

Claudia threw a couch pillow at her.

"Roy's not exactly a hot number," I agreed.

"Your mother wouldn't care about that," Mallory said.

"I'm not saying she's shallow, just human." I gave Roy a thumbs-down.

Kristy, Mallory, and Mary Anne said thumbs-up. Claudia and I agreed on thumbs-down.

I clicked off the video. "Trust me. My mother would not want to date him."

"Then which one would she like?" Kristy asked, sounding frustrated.

"None of them," I said. "Sorry." I turned to Claudia. "It was a great idea, really. And the way you got the tape was brilliant. I just don't see anyone there who would be right for Mom. I hope you're not mad."

"No, I'm not mad. I didn't see any good matches for her there either. But one thing still bothers me."

"What?" I asked.

Claudia sighed. "What do we do now?"

Chapter 9

By the time I came home from my BSC meeting that afternoon I felt defeated.

My friends and I had spent every spare minute discussing my mother — and no one had thought of a way to cheer her up.

As I headed toward the kitchen, I heard singing. Mom had left the radio on.

I stopped. No. *Mom* was singing!

She sounded awfully happy.

I continued into the kitchen. Her back was to me as she unpacked a bag of groceries. Her song was one I'd heard on one of her albums, called "Feelin' Groovy."

And, obviously, she was feelin' groovy.

She whipped out a cereal box from the bag and

tossed it from hand to hand before landing it on a shelf in the cupboard.

I coughed to let her know I was there.

She turned and smiled. "Hi," she said, not even embarrassed that I'd seen her acting so goofy.

"Hi," I replied. "Did something good happen?"

"I got tired of being gloomy. It's spring. Everything is basically fine, so why should I be down?"

Because Dad's getting married, I thought, *and that's upsetting you. Because you're lonely.* But I was glad she was smiling.

She held a jar out to me. "I picked up that ranch dip you like," she said. "There are some cut-up veggies in the fridge."

I took the jar from her. "Thanks." I found the vegetables and brought them to the kitchen table along with the dip. She joined me while I ate.

"How was your day?" she asked.

I told her about the main events — a science test, a special presentation by the glee club in the auditorium, Alan Gray waiting for Claudia at her locker.

I left out the part about screening possible dates for her.

"How was your day?" I asked when I was done.

"Not bad," she said, smiling. "Busy. I went into Stamford to look at a preview of fall clothing. Can you believe they're bringing those things out already? Every year it's the same, but it always seems so insane."

"You like those previews, though," I said. Was that all it took to restore her good mood?

"I do, it's true. It gives me a chance to chat with buyers from other stores whom I've gotten to know over the years. A bunch of us even went to lunch together."

"That must have been fun."

"It was. Lots of fun." As she spoke, she took a catalog from the pile of mail that lay on the table. I ate while she flipped through it.

After a moment, she slid the open catalog over to me. "Do you think I'd look good in that?"

It was a color photo of a woman wearing a dark pink wrap dress that tied at the side. "You'd look great in it," I said. "But it's kind of fancy. Where would you wear it?"

"Out to dinner?"

"Definitely, if you were going to a really nice place," I replied. "Are you . . . going to a nice place?"

"I think so. It's a dinner dance at a country club, so it should be pretty fancy."

A dinner dance! At a country club! What was this?

"With who?" I asked.

"One of the buyers. He works for a huge chain of department stores, and apparently they throw a big dinner dance every year. So today at lunch he asked me to go with him."

"But who is this guy?"

"His name is Gabriel Dillon. He's a very nice man. He's asked me out before but I just wasn't ready to date at the time. Now I figured, what the heck?"

"Good for you! When's the dance?"

"This Saturday."

"Saturday! Cool!" I cried. I was glad it was soon and not months away. "Wait a minute. Saturday's no good."

"Why not?"

"I won't be here. I'll be in Manhattan. If I'm not here, who will help you get dressed?"

Mom chuckled. "Stacey, I've been dressing myself for years, even before you were born. I think I know a little about fashion. It is my business, after all."

"I know, Mom, but you're too timid. You won't wear enough makeup. You'll go light on the jewelry.

You're afraid to really show how beautiful you are."

"Well, thank you, I think. We'll do a practice run before you leave. How's that?"

"Okay," I agreed. "And don't order that dress. We'll go shopping for one that is just the right color and fits you great. You'll want to try it on."

"If you say so." She stretched her fingers in front of her face and examined her nails. "I'll need a manicure. A pedicure too, since I'm planning to wear open-toed shoes. And I'll want to have my hair done that day."

What good luck! I was so happy that Gabriel guy had asked her out. Perfect timing.

Her good mood lasted about a day and a half. We shopped together later that evening. I picked out a gorgeous blue dress that shimmered when it moved.

Mom tried it on and looked amazing.

"I'd never have picked this on my own, Stacey," she said, twirling in front of the store mirror. "But it's just perfect. What would I do without you?"

That's what I was wondering.

By Thursday afternoon she'd stopped humming and singing. A nervous expression had replaced her smile.

That evening, she went out for her manicure and pedicure. When she returned, she spent the rest of the night fretting that the rose-colored polish she'd selected was too bright.

"It's going to be beautiful with the dress," I assured her.

"Who will even notice the dress with these neon nails blinding them?"

I sighed. "They're not even close to neon. Stop worrying."

By Friday, it would be accurate to say she was a nervous wreck. "If Judy's not there tomorrow, I'm not letting anyone else do my hair," she said.

"You made the appointment with Judy. She'll be there," I told her, looking up from the TV.

"What if she's sick?"

"Then someone else will do it."

"No one else there can cut like Judy can. They'll ruin my hair, and I refuse to go to a dinner dance with strangers if I'm looking terrible."

"That won't happen. You're worrying over nothing. Why do you think Judy might be sick?"

"I don't know. There's a terrible cold going around. Two people called in sick today at work."

"Mom, you need to chill," I told her as kindly as I could. "You're making yourself crazy."

"I know I am." She sat on the couch and took a deep breath. "It's not like I'm madly in love with Gabe either. It's just that I haven't been out with anyone in so long. I'll calm down." She drew in a deep breath. "Okay. I'm okay now."

"Good," I said. "You'll be fine."

"I know I will. I only wish I hadn't gotten this manicure so soon. I'm bound to chip one of these nails by tomorrow. Maybe I should wear gloves to protect my nails until tomorrow." She stood up again and headed out of the room. "I know I have a pair of rubber gloves somewhere," she said to herself as she left. "They're probably under the sink."

Man, oh, man! Was she nervous! Did she actually plan on walking around in rubber gloves until the next night?

And what was she going to do about her pedicure? Wear scuba flippers?

Mom came back to the living room holding the rubber gloves. "I bet your father wasn't this nervous when he first met Samantha," she said.

"Who knows," I said with a shrug of my shoulders.

"You're right. It doesn't matter how he felt. This is about me, not him. Who cares?"

"Right."

"Right," she echoed.

I hoped Mom wasn't going to act this nervous on Saturday night, or her date was going to be a disaster.

Chapter 10

By eleven that Saturday morning I was in Manhattan, but my mind was back in Stoneybrook.

Once again, I met Ethan at Grand Central Station. "You seem anxious about something," he observed right away.

"I am," I admitted, and told him about Mom's big date.

"She'll be okay," Ethan reassured me.

"If they were only going to a movie, I don't think she'd be so freaked," I told him. "But she won't know anyone else at this thing, and it's so fancy and all. I shouldn't be so far away when she needs me."

"But there's nothing you can do about it. Even if you were home, you couldn't go *on* the date with her."

The idea of it — my tagging along to the country club — was so silly it made me laugh. "I know."

"Yeah, so forget it. Everything will be okay."

I did forget about Mom for awhile. Ethan and I ate some bagels and talked. At noon, Ethan left and Dad came to meet me. We were on our way up the stairs when I noticed the time.

"Dad, I need to make a call," I told him as I fished my cell phone from my bag.

He frowned. "To whom?"

"Mom," I said, punching in our number. I knew she'd be home from the hairdresser by now. "Mom, it's Stacey," I said when she picked up. "Was Judy there?"

She was, and Mom was pretty pleased with her hair, although she was afraid it might be a little too short.

"It'll look great once you get your makeup and earrings on," I said. "I hope you didn't wear those rubber gloves to the salon."

She said she hadn't. Besides, she'd found matching polish, so if she chipped a nail, she could repair it.

"Is that over with?" Dad asked after I hung up.

"Yup."

"Where's your mother going?"

"To a dinner dance."

"Sounds pretty special," he said as we stepped outside and he hailed a cab.

"I guess it is."

To my surprise, he told the driver to take us uptown to the Metropolitan Museum instead of going back to the apartment. "The Versace show is back," he explained. "I know you were disappointed you'd missed it before, so I was pretty sure you'd want to catch it this time."

"Definitely!" I cried. Before he died, Gianni Versace designed the coolest clothing. Gorgeous gowns. Hip outfits. Lots of famous people wear them. "I can't believe you remembered," I said, truly impressed.

"Well, to be honest," he said, "I didn't. Samantha knew you'd missed the show and she suggested going today."

Somehow, that was even better than Dad's remembering. It meant Samantha was starting to include me in her thoughts, in her life. I liked the idea.

When the cab pulled up in front of the museum I spotted Samantha right away. She stood on the wide front steps dressed in black pants, a bright white T-shirt, and dark sunglasses. Her hair was pulled back from her face with a red scarf. I wondered if Dad had felt nervous when he first asked her out.

We climbed out of the cab and joined her. "Thanks for remembering that I wanted to see this," I said.

"You'll love it," she replied. "I saw it the last time."

I loved that Samantha and I had things in common.

"After Versace, want to go upstairs and see the Degas ballerinas?" Samantha asked.

"I'd love to!" I told her. "I've seen them a million times but I never get tired of them."

"Me neither. Those paintings bring me right into that world."

"Would you ladies mind if I pass on the gowns?" Dad spoke up. "I could go to the armor collection and meet you up at Degas."

"Fine with me," Samantha agreed.

"Me too," I said. It would interesting to spend some time alone with Samantha.

In the crowded high-ceilinged lobby, we split up. Samantha and I went down a flight of steps to reach the exhibit. The gowns were displayed on faceless mannequins in glass cases.

I recognized some of the dresses from pictures in celebrity magazines. I'd seen a photo of Elizabeth Hurley in one of them, attending some event with Hugh Grant. I also remembered a magazine cover with Princess Diana wearing another of the dresses.

"It's amazing to see these for real," I said to Samantha as we gazed into the cases.

"The fabrics are just gorgeous," she commented.

We took our time, lingering over each dress. Samantha didn't seem to want to rush, and neither did I. I was having too much fun.

Which made me feel guilty.

Here I was, having a good time with Dad's wife-to-be, while my mother was home alone in a state of panic.

"Excuse me, I'll be right back," I said to Samantha. I stepped into the stairwell and took out my cell phone. The phone began doing strange things. It said I was roaming. Then it gave me a busy signal.

Stupid phone. I needed to talk to my mother. I wasn't sure if it was for her sake or for mine. I just knew I had to speak to her right away.

I canceled the call and tried again. The phone gave me another busy signal. That was weird, because we have call waiting. Unless Mom was on the Internet — something she doesn't do much — she should be picking up.

I canceled the call and tried yet again. This time the phone showed some strange error message. I was so busy trying to make the phone work I didn't realize Samantha had joined me.

"It's very hard to call out of here on a cell phone," she said. "The walls are incredibly thick, plus we're underground right now. If the call is really urgent you can go upstairs to use a pay phone."

I thought a moment. Was the call urgent? Or did my guilt over being with Samantha today just make me feel as if it were?

"I guess it's not super-important," I admitted, slipping the phone back into my bag. "Mom has a date and she's nervous. I wanted to check in and see how she was."

"That's sweet of you," Samantha said. "I'm sure she'll be all right, though. She's a strong woman. She can handle herself."

What she said was true. Mom is a very capable

person. I forget that sometimes, because she shows me the softer, more vulnerable side of her personality that she hides from other people.

But how did Samantha know that? Did Dad talk about Mom? Was it because Mom had called to congratulate them on their engagement?

Whatever the reason, it was nice of her to say so.

"That's true," I agreed. "She knows what she's doing."

"Ready for Degas?" asked Samantha. "Your dad is probably wondering what happened to us."

We found Dad on a bench by the Degas paintings, looking extremely bored. "I thought maybe you were trying on the gowns," he teased when we joined him.

"Wouldn't that be great!" I said.

We looked at the paintings a little faster than we might have if Dad hadn't been with us.

Next, at Dad's request, we went through the new Greek antiquities section. To me, it's not the most thrilling part of the museum but going to the exhibit was only fair since Dad had gone to Degas.

"How about an early supper? The museum restaurant is pretty good," Dad suggested when we were done.

"Could we go somewhere outside the museum?"

I asked. The truth was, I was dying to get someplace where I could use my phone.

Samantha must have known what I was thinking. “You really don’t have to worry,” she said softly.

I sighed and hoped she was right.

Chapter 11

I had a hard time sleeping that night. I wanted to know how Mom's evening had been. I lay in bed imagining every possible thing that could have gone wrong — from Mom's hem ripping to her date's turning out to be a big jerk.

After I finally did fall asleep, I kept waking up and checking my digital clock. Sometimes only a half hour had passed since the last time I'd awakened.

It was torture.

At about three o'clock, my eyes popped open yet again, and I actually considered calling Mom. But finally I forced myself to roll over and shut my eyes. And I stayed asleep. I dreamed Mom and Dad were sitting on a bench in Central Park talking, but they were speaking gibberish, which I couldn't understand. I kept asking them what they were talking about, but they just smiled at me.

That dream was still in my head when Dad gently shook me awake at 9:15.

"Come on, we're going to check out the Starstruck Diner, the one we read about," he said.

Sleepily, I opened my eyes. "Oh, yeah, I remember."

My restless night had left me tired. With an effort, I sat up. I wanted to flop down again, but I forced myself to stay upright.

"What happened to your restaurant rule? You know — once a restaurant has been written up in the paper, it's too crowded to get into for at least a month," I said.

"Well, Samantha's dying to go. We're hoping that if we get there a little early, we'll beat the crowd."

Hmm. He was being very flexible. Samantha was managing to loosen him up.

"Okay, cool," I said, swinging my legs to the floor. "I'm always up for checking out a new restaurant."

Dad left and I dressed quickly in khakis, sandals, and a short-sleeved sweater with bands of color that faded from dark to light green.

I found Samantha in the living room, sitting on the couch, reading *The New York Times*. "Nice sweater," she commented as I emerged from my room.

"Thanks. I'm really excited about this restaurant," I told her.

"Me too. It's more of a diner, but it's a cool diner. I hear they make fabulous caviar omelets."

I wrinkled my nose. "I'm not big on caviar, but I bet I'll find plenty I like."

The three of us took a cab to the diner. If we thought we'd beat the crowd we were sorely mistaken. The line outside the place was already halfway down the block.

"I'll bet it moves quickly," Samantha said as we climbed out of the cab. Dad didn't look so sure. To my surprise, though, he didn't object.

Personally, I wasn't starving. I'd prepared for the possibility of a line by having a banana before we left. And it was a nice morning. I didn't mind waiting. I considered calling Mom but figured I'd give her a little longer to sleep.

I was in the middle of my favorite thing to do while in line — people watching — when someone called my name.

The voice had come from the beginning of the

line. I strained to see over heads, but didn't spot anyone I knew. Then a girl with a long mane of brown curls and large brown eyes stepped out of line and I realized who she was. "Laine!" I cried without stopping to decide if I really wanted to talk to her.

In the next second, I realized I felt incredibly awkward about running into her. I had no choice but to put a smile on my face, though.

Laine Cummings used to be my very best friend when I lived in Manhattan. We'd been friends from the time we were five, and by age eight, we were super-best friends. My moving to Stoneybrook, though, put a huge strain on our friendship — so huge that we weren't friends anymore. We'd both tried, at least at first. Laine visited me, but she didn't mix well with my Stoneybrook friends. She didn't like them, and she made her feelings pretty clear. So naturally my friends didn't like her either. Laine and I hadn't talked, or seen each other, or even written in a long time.

Now, here she was. Right in front of me.

Laine seemed happy to see me, so I acted happy to see her.

And, in a way, I was. She was part of my past.

Laine wrapped me in a quick, tight hug. She smelled like jasmine, a fragrance she never used to wear. "How are you?" she asked, as if nothing had gone wrong between us.

"Good. How are you?"

"Awesome. I'm here with my friends." She jerked her head back toward the spot she'd come from. I saw a bunch of kids around my age, some older. Boys and girls both. I didn't know any of them, though. "What's new?" she asked.

I gave her the quick version of my recent life. When I told her about my fight with Claudia, she rolled her eyes. "I never liked her — too much with the art and not too bright."

Her remark didn't surprise me. I knew Laine had particularly disliked Claudia from the start. She was jealous, I guess.

"Oh, Claudia's smart in her own way," I said.

"Yeah, but I'd have dumped her for a guy too."

I hated the way she made that sound. "It wasn't like that at all," I said. "It would probably take too long to explain, though. Anyhow, she and I are friends again and neither of us sees the guy we were fighting over."

"He was probably a jerk."

"No, he wasn't. He was pretty nice. It just didn't work out," I said.

Talking to Laine was even more uncomfortable

than I had imagined it might be. Things didn't flow smoothly at all. And Laine even looked tough, with heavy dark blue eyeliner ringing her eyes and black nail polish.

"What's been happening with you?" I asked.

"Same old same old. King and I broke up, though. He was getting to be a real pain. School's a drag, but the kids are fun. Want to join us?"

"I can't. I'm here with Dad and his girlfriend, Samantha."

Laine noticed Dad and Samantha for the first time. "Oh, hi, Mr. McGill. How are you?"

"Fine, Laine. Nice to see you. How are your parents?"

Laine shrugged. "Fine, I guess. I'll tell them you said hi. Can Stacey come sit with us?"

Dad seemed undecided. Taking a step behind Laine, so she couldn't see me, I shook my head, signaling Dad to say no. Samantha smiled but quickly looked away so Laine wouldn't notice.

"If you don't mind, Laine, we have some plans to make," Dad fibbed. "I'm sure you girls can get together another time."

"Absolutely," Laine agreed. "It's been way too long, Stacey. Call me, okay? Do you still have my number?"

"I have it," I replied, which was true. It was still in my phone book.

Laine hugged me again. "Don't forget. Call me."

I nodded, even though I was pretty sure I would never call her.

Laine waved as she rejoined her friends. I was relieved to see her go. I had known we were through being friends the last time I'd seen her. Now, though, it was as if we were from different planets.

Still . . . she was Laine. Behind all that eyeliner and mascara were the same eyes that had lit up with laughter when I told her one of my corny jokes.

A tide of memories flooded me.

Getting soaked with artificial movie rain as Laine and I watched a film being made on a street downtown.

The two of us climbing in the ductwork of my building to spy on neighbors — both of us unable to stop giggling.

Crying in Laine's bedroom because my parents were fighting again.

Walking together on the beach the time she came on vacation with Mom and me.

A few days ago, Claudia had presented me with a riddle. "What does everyone collect whether they want to or not?" I didn't know. "Memories" was the answer.

That's when it hit me.

The way I felt about Laine was probably the way Mom felt about Dad. She didn't want to live her life with him anymore, but she had a bundle of good memories. Such as eating clams with Dad. And now that Dad was marrying Samantha, something in Mom's life was over. There was no longer any possibility of turning back to it.

How would I feel if Laine had told me she was moving to Australia and I'd never be able to see her again? Probably the way Mom was feeling now.

I opened my bag to search for my phone, but the diner line suddenly surged forward and I had to move with it. We were seated pretty quickly after that. Somehow it didn't seem right to sit at the table with Samantha and Dad while I called Mom to ask about her date.

Still, I was dying to find out, and to tell her that I now understood how she felt.

❀ Chapter 12

Finally, after brunch (which was awesome), I couldn't stand it another second. I excused myself from the table and headed toward the ladies' room. Instead of going in, I stood outside and phoned Mom.

"It's me," I said when she answered. "How was it?"

A pause. It made me nervous.

"Not great."

"But not terrible?" I asked hopefully.

Another pause.

"Let's just say I'm pretty sure Gabe and I won't be having a second date."

"Why? What happened?" Had he upset her? Been rude? Thoughtless? "What did he do?"

"He was fine. A perfect gentleman. We just could not keep up a conversation for more than five minutes. There was no connection between us. Basically, we sat there and stared at each other the whole evening."

"Did you dance, at least?" I asked.

"He doesn't dance."

"You went to a dinner dance with a guy who doesn't dance? How awful." I could picture her sitting there, looking beautiful, having the most boring, disappointing evening imaginable. "Was the food any good?"

"Passable," she answered dully.

"Gosh, Mom, I'm sorry it was such a bummer. Are you okay?"

"Yes. Of course," she replied. Only she didn't sound okay.

"I'll be home as soon as I can."

"Don't rush," she said. "How's your weekend going?"

"Okay." It wasn't the right time to rave about the Versace show; the movie Dad, Samantha, and I had seen the night before; or the great brunch this morning. "I ran into Laine Cummings," I added. "It was weird seeing her."

"Hmmm. I know how that can be."

"Mom, I love you," I said. "I'll be there soon. 'Bye."

"Okay. Again, don't rush on my account. 'Bye."

I *was* going to rush on her account. She needed me. I should have stayed home this weekend. But I hadn't, so now I needed to get back as fast as possible.

Hurrying back to the table, I saw Dad paying the check. "There's a concert in the park this afternoon," he said when he saw me. "I thought we could head over there and — "

"Do you mind if I just go home?" I asked.

"I guess not. What's the big hurry?"

"Mom," I explained. I almost launched into the story of her disastrous date, but I stopped myself. It seemed disloyal to talk to Dad and Samantha about the private conversation between Mom and me.

"She doesn't feel well," I said instead. This was almost true. Mom had certainly felt better than she was feeling today, even if she wasn't actually sick. "She told me not to rush home, but I didn't like the way she sounded," I added. I didn't want them to think Mom had asked me to come home to take care of her.

Dad and Samantha exchanged a look. I couldn't tell what it meant — probably that they suspected there was more to the story than I was telling.

"I'll drive you," Samantha offered.

Dad and I looked at her in surprise. She'd never offered to drive me anywhere before. I didn't even know she had a car.

"But the concert," Dad objected. "It was your idea to — "

"I only thought Stacey would like it," Samantha cut in. "If she's not going to be here I don't mind if I miss it. It's such a gorgeous day, I wouldn't mind getting out of the city."

"I'll come too, then," Dad said.

Samantha held up her hand. "There's no need, Ed. I know you have work to catch up on."

"True," Dad agreed.

I smiled to myself. Dad *always* had work to catch up on. Samantha had already learned the perfect way to distract him.

She put her napkin on the table and patted my hand. "This way we'll spend some time together, and your mom won't have to pick you up at the station, since she's not feeling well."

"That would be great," I said. The train takes about a half hour longer than a car ride. "Dad, is it okay if I just leave the rest of my stuff at your place?"

"Of course."

We left the diner, and Samantha and I took a cab

to the garage where her car is parked. Soon we were heading out of the city. Samantha pushed a button and the sunroof slid back, letting in sunlight and a cool breeze.

"This will be nice. We'll have some time to talk," she said. "Just you and me."

"That was cool the way you convinced Dad to stay home," I commented.

Samantha laughed. "You can always convince a workaholic to work. It's pretty easy."

"Do you mind that he works so much?" I asked.

"No, not at all. I'm a bit of a workaholic myself."

It occurred to me that I didn't know what Samantha did for a living. She rarely spoke about it, so I assumed it wasn't a very important part of her life. "What do you do?" I asked.

"Fashion photography," she said.

Wow! That was so cool. So that was why she was so interested in the Versace exhibit. "I've never heard you mention it. If I were doing something that awesome I'd be talking about it every second."

Samantha smiled. "When I'm not working, I try to put work out of my mind. If I think about it all the time, then I'm working twenty-four hours a day. And I don't think that's healthy. Your father and I have talked about it and he's trying not to make work his life too."

"He's much better than he used to be," I told her. "Nothing Mom did could make him change."

"Maybe he listens to me because we're so much alike. Or maybe now he wants to change, since he knows that his work habits cost him his marriage."

What she said was probably true. But I didn't want to talk about it anymore. Why couldn't he have realized these things *before* they cost him his marriage?

I changed the subject. "Do you travel a lot?" I asked.

"All the time. I'm headed for Alaska next week."

"Cool! I've always wanted to see Alaska."

"Cool is the point," said Samantha. "It's hard to believe, but we're shooting fall fashion already and we wanted a background that still looks wintry. We'll travel by cruise ship and I'll shoot from the deck, with the snowy mountains in the background."

"What a great career. How did you get into it?" I asked.

"I was a model for awhile," she said. "But as I got older, I was less in demand, so I turned to something I also knew pretty well by then, photography."

I had a million questions about the fashion industry. "You can come on a shoot with me sometime," Samantha offered when we were close to Stamford.

"That would be great!" I said, barely able to believe it might be true. "I would adore that!"

"Good. When I come back from Alaska, I'll work on setting it up."

I pointed out the Stoneybrook exit then and Samantha turned off the highway. In minutes I was in familiar surroundings again — and it felt all wrong to be in the car with Samantha.

It was like being with my mother, only I was with the wrong mother. I squirmed in my seat.

Then I pointed out my school and my friends' houses, hoping Samantha wouldn't pick up on my anxiety. She had driven me all this way. And I didn't know what to do with her now.

I couldn't invite her inside when I got home. That was all Mom needed.

"Want to see some more of Stoneybrook?" I asked.

"Sure. I've heard so much about it. I'm very curious."

I guided her to the Stoneybrook Museum, the civic center, the library, and the community center.

"You travel back and forth between two very different worlds," she commented.

I nodded. "I hope you don't mind, but I really should get home," I said. "You know . . . with Mom not feeling well and all."

"Absolutely. You'll have to guide me there, though." I gave her directions and soon we pulled up in front of my house.

"Thanks so much," I said, getting out of the car.

"You're welcome. I hope your mother feels better." With a smile and a wave, she took off.

I watched her drive down the street. She was so nice, and she was perfect for my father. Now that she was heading back to the city, I could feel good about her again.

And I did.

Chapter 13

"Stacey, you don't have to cheer me up, really," Mom insisted. We were sitting in the living room late that afternoon and I was trying, desperately, to keep up a lively conversation.

"I wasn't trying to cheer you up," I fibbed. "I just thought you'd want to hear about a chimp who liked to dress in a tuxedo and attend weddings. When I saw it on TV I laughed so hard I could hardly stand it."

"You probably had to see it to get the full impact."

"Maybe."

Earlier, when I'd come home, I'd asked Mom if she wanted to talk about her date, but she said she'd rather just forget it. She claimed she was tired from being out late, but one look at her face told me she was depressed.

I sighed. The chimp story was the last funny thing I could think of. What else could I do to lift her spirits?

"Mallory called this morning," Mom said, suddenly remembering. "Why don't you try cheering *her* up? She sounded sort of sad."

"I wasn't trying to cheer you up!" I said again as I went to the phone and punched in Mallory's number.

"Hi, it's Stacey. What's up?" I said when Mallory answered.

"Are you doing anything today?" she asked.

I looked at Mom. She'd begun doing the Sunday *New York Times* crossword puzzle. That might take up most of the afternoon, and she didn't exactly seem to be craving my company.

"I guess not," I replied. "What did you have in mind?"

"Want to come over?"

"Okay."

I hung up and told Mom I was going to the Pikes' house. "Have fun," she said, barely looking up from her puzzle.

I cut through our yards to Mallory's. She was waiting on the back steps. "Hi," she said. "I don't even want my brothers and sisters to know you're here. They might want your attention and I don't feel like dealing with them right now."

"That bad?"

"They're just driving me crazy," she said. I followed her to the picnic table in the backyard. "Everything still feels so strange around here. I wish I were back at Riverbend."

"Really? You're not glad to be home in Stoneybrook, even a little?"

"I'm happy to see everybody, but I don't feel like I fit in anymore. Nothing's the way it was."

"I think I know what you mean," I said, taking a seat beside her. "This morning I saw Laine, my old friend."

"I remember her."

"She's changed, and so much time has passed. I didn't know what to say to her. It was totally awkward."

"Believe me, I understand!" Mallory said. "That's exactly how I feel. It's just the same."

I thought about it a moment. Was it the same?

"I don't think so," I said.

"Why not?"

"Well, for one thing, Laine and I had a fight the last time I saw her. But today she acted as if everything were fine between us — when it wasn't. You're still friends with everyone here, though. We've been e-mailing back and forth all this time."

Mallory threw her arms up in frustration. "Then why do I feel so distant from everyone?"

"You're too impatient," I told her. "Once school is out everyone will have more free time. We're all looking forward to spending the summer with you, Mal. You know how crazy spring gets. There are exams and recitals and all kinds of end-of-term things. It's probably the worst possible time to come back from school."

"You think?"

"Definitely. If you came back home in July everyone would be all over you."

"That's nice of you to say." Mallory slumped down on the picnic bench so that her head rested on her hands. "But it's not just that everyone else seems different, it's that *I* feel different too. So much happened to me at Riverbend. I've changed a lot this year. But I don't know how to explain it. My friends and family are treating me as if I were the person who left — and I'm not that person any longer."

"What kinds of things happened?" I asked.

"Well, take the Internet Club, for example," she began. "A lot of the girls at Riverbend didn't know how to use the Internet. So I went to the computer teacher and asked her if we could get together one night a week in the computer room so she could show us how to get onto different Web sites, do research, and stuff like that."

"Cool," I said.

"Yeah, it was. And since I already knew more than most of the girls, I wound up assisting the teacher and being voted president of the club."

"Hey, that's great!"

"Me, Mallory Pike. The president of something!"

I thought how down on herself Mallory had felt before she left for Riverbend. She'd had a couple of unpleasant experiences at school and some kids were making fun of her. Riverbend had obviously been exactly what she needed to build her self-esteem.

"That's really cool," I said.

"I know. But I can't seem to share it with people here," she complained.

"You're sharing it with me."

Slowly, a smile spread across her face. "That's true, isn't it? I did just share it with you. But no one else will be interested. Or they'll just think I'm bragging."

"Your friends will want to hear all about it."

"Really? Because I could let you know all about what we did. I found some computer Web sites that were really useful."

"Definitely!" I said.

As Mallory spoke, I realized that she was showing me a side of herself I hadn't seen much of before. Before she left for Riverbend, she was hardly ever in the lead. That was probably because, at eleven, she's younger than most of us. But I always assumed it was part of her personality to hang back.

It was natural, though, for her to be a leader. After all, despite what Adam, Jordan, and especially Byron might think, she is the oldest of eight kids. That had put her in the leadership position almost from the beginning of her life.

I could see it had been good for her to get away from us, especially from Kristy, who is so overpowering sometimes. And maybe even from Jessi, who was so accomplished at dancing that Mallory was a little in her shadow. At Riverbend Mallory had been able to shine.

Only now she was expected to become Mallory the sidekick again, Mallory the follower, the one in the background. Even her role as oldest child was being challenged.

"You know, I think I'm beginning to understand how you feel," I told her. "You just can't accept everyone's idea of who you are. You have to let them know things have changed."

"Change is so hard," she grumbled.

I groaned and tossed my head back, thinking of all the changes in my life recently. "Tell me about it," I said.

Then I thought about Dad's upcoming marriage, and my new, better relationship with Ethan, and I smiled.

"But you can't stop it," I added. "And some things change for the better."

Chapter 14

On Monday afternoon I was happy to see Mallory at our BSC meeting. She was there front and center. She had ideas about how we could organize a trip to the Stoneybrook Museum for the kids we sit for. And she'd printed out a list of things to do that she'd found on a Connecticut Web site.

"Awesome," Kristy murmured, nodding. I could see she was impressed.

Mallory beamed. "Thanks. And this is something I could even do from Riverbend. I could e-mail you information I find on Web sites."

"Does the school give you total access to the Internet?" I asked.

"No. But we can get into travel and informational sites without any problem."

The entire meeting had an upbeat feel to it, and

Mallory was responsible for that. She had set the tone. I picked up a few sitting jobs for the coming week and headed home feeling good.

To be honest, I also felt good about myself for having helped Mallory assert herself.

Outside my house, I stopped for a moment and prepared to go in. I wondered if I should seem so cheery when Mom was in the dumps. Then I decided — what the heck — maybe being around a cheerful person was exactly what Mom needed right now.

The radio was blasting in the kitchen, a rhythm and blues song sung by Aretha Franklin. It's the one in which she spells out the word *respect.* On my way to the kitchen I had to pass by the dining room. It surprised me to see that the table was beautifully set for two.

"Is someone coming over?" I asked Mom as I entered the kitchen. Something delicious-smelling was cooking in a big pot.

Mom smiled at me as she tossed some chopped vegetables into it. "Nope. Just me and you. I was in the mood to have a nice dinner, that's all."

I stared at her. Something about her was different. For one thing, she seemed awfully happy. And her hair looked as if it had been professionally blown-dry. But she was wearing jeans and a T-shirt.

Usually at this hour she's still in her work outfit. "Did you go to work today?" I asked.

"Nope. I took the day off."

"Why?"

"Felt like it."

This worried me.

My expression must have told her I was concerned. "Don't worry. I have personal days coming to me. I'm entitled to take some time off. It's not a problem. I needed the day to think and to make some phone calls."

"What's up?"

She waved me away. "Not now. I've made some decisions, but I want to tell you at dinner."

"Okay," I agreed cautiously.

"You have a message from Ethan on the computer," Mom went on. "I'll call you when dinner is ready."

"Want some help?"

"Thank you, but I'm all set. Go see what Ethan wanted."

I sat down at the computer in the family room and went on-line to check my e-mail. There was Ethan's message.

Hi, Stace,

School ends for me in two weeks and so does my

artists' studio class. I'll be working at the gallery this summer, but I don't think I'll be taking summer classes. (Don't have the cash right now.)

I just picked up the schedule for the free concerts in the park and there are some awesome acts playing. Also, Shakespeare in the Park features some big names this summer.

You'll notice I'm tuned into free stuff right now (the same no-cash issue), but I think we can still have a pretty good time on the cheap.

When you know your city schedule, send me a message and I'll make some plans.

Ethan

I hit the reply button and wrote him back. I still wasn't sure which weekends I'd be in the city, but I'd let him know as soon as I planned things with Mom and Dad. Then I wrote him about Mom's date — how it was a bust, but that she was happy about something mysterious now.

I'll tell you what it is when I find out myself, I wrote. I sent the message and logged off.

I went upstairs to do some homework. It was hard to keep my mind on it, though. I was too busy wondering what Mom's big decisions might be. Maybe they were really, really big. What if she wanted to move to some place far away . . . such as

Japan? Sure, it would be exciting, but it was the last thing I wanted.

Or what if she'd decided to sell all our possessions and go off to India to aid the poor? It would be admirable, but I didn't think I was unselfish enough to make that step.

By the time Mom called me for dinner, I was plenty worried. Exactly what did she have in mind? But as I came down the stairs my mouth began to water. I found a gorgeous, fragrant chicken fricassee sitting in the middle of the table next to a green salad.

Mom came out of the kitchen with a bottle of mineral water. "Mom, you have to tell me what's going on right away or I'll burst!" I exclaimed.

"All right. Sit down."

I couldn't. I was too anxious to sit.

"Here's my first decision, and I hope you'll be okay with it."

I held my breath and waited.

"I'm going back to my original name."

I didn't understand. "What name?"

"Spencer. My last name before I married your father."

I collapsed into the chair as relief rushed over me.

"I know it's a bit of a shock," she went on. "We

won't have the same name and that might be a problem. Can you deal with it?"

"Of course. Do you know how many kids at school have a different last name than one of their parents? Or both of them?"

"A lot?" she asked, sounding hopeful.

"A ton. It could be half, maybe even more. It's sort of confusing, but everyone deals with it."

Mom placed her hand over her heart, smiling. "I am so relieved to hear that. It makes sense, of course, what with divorce, remarriage, and women keeping their own names to begin with."

"What made you decide to do it?" I asked.

"A number of things. For one, soon there will be another Mrs. McGill."

I wondered if Samantha would change her name. Somehow I just couldn't picture her becoming Mrs. McGill. She was so much Samantha Young.

I suppose that was what Mom was after — she wanted people to think of her as Maureen Spencer, her own self, not Mrs. Somebody. Or Mrs. *Any*body.

"I don't *feel* like Mrs. McGill anymore," Mom continued. "It's not who I am, it's who I was."

I remembered Mallory making the distinction between who she was before Riverbend and who she was now.

"I think I understand," I said.

"It's okay, then?" Mom asked.

"Completely okay." The aroma of the chicken was making me hungry. "Can we eat now?"

"In a second," she said. "I have another announcement, and this is really the bigger one."

My breath caught in my throat. Uh-oh. Here it came. I had relaxed too soon. I was about to go off to live in Japan with Ms. Spencer.

"I'm seriously thinking of quitting my job," said Mom.

Cringing, I waited for the rest of the announcement.

"And I'd like to open my own clothing shop here in Stoneybrook."

"Right here?" I cried excitedly. "Your *own*?"

"Yes, I'm looking at some empty storefronts for rent. That's one of the things I did today. I also went to the bank and spoke to a representative there about getting a new-business loan."

I leaped out of my chair, knocking it over. I felt as if springs were attached to the soles of my feet as I jumped up and down. "Yes! Yes! Yes!"

"Calm down," Mom said, laughter in her voice. "It might not even happen. I have to get approval on the loan, for one thing."

"You'll get it." Mom was meant to do this. I knew she could. It would be so much more fun than working in boring old Bellair's.

"I could work in the store with you after school and summers," I volunteered immediately. "You could carry junior sizes as well as adult. All my friends would come."

"Wouldn't that be great?" Mom said. "You know, Stacey, I want this a lot. It's been on my mind for a long time."

"Is that what you were thinking about the night Claudia came over and we made pizza?"

Mom's eyes widened in surprise. "Yes, it was. How did you know I had something on my mind that night?"

"I could tell," I said. "You know, I always think that you know me better than anyone else does. I guess I know you too."

Mom reached for my hand and squeezed it. "It's wonderful to have someone who really knows you, don't you think?" I nodded. "You've been such a great support to me, Stacey," Mom added. "I suppose that's not the way it should be. A parent should be there for the child, not the other way around. I'll try not to put you in that position again. But I want you to know that I appreciate how wonderful you've been through all this."

"Thanks," I said.

Mom leaned back in her chair. "I'm going to do this. No matter what it takes. The good times are about to start again, Stacey. I'm sure of it."

Chapter 15

"Serious Clothing," Kristy suggested. "There's a name that says it all."

"No way!" Claudia cried, making a disgusted face. "I'd never go into a store with that name. How about Funky Petunia?"

"No one over twenty would go into a store named Funky Petunia," said Mary Anne. "I think she should call it Amazing Grace."

"That's nice," I agreed.

I'd invited everyone to my house for a slumber party after our BSC meeting that Friday. Once again, we made a pizza, only this time we used store-bought pizza dough and jars of sauce. Mom was much too busy now to make those things from scratch.

She'd had a hectic week since her announcement to me on Monday. Every night she came in late because she'd been scouting locations, or talking with someone at the bank, or meeting with clothing suppliers to see what kinds of deals she could make. Tonight she was seeing an accountant.

There was a knock at the side door. Kristy answered it and let in Mallory and Jessi. They tossed their sleeping bags onto a kitchen chair. "Wow, that looks good. I'm starved!" Jessi said, catching sight of the two half-made pizzas on the table.

Mom came in right behind them. "Hi, girls," she said brightly.

"Hi, Mrs. . . . um, Mrs. . . ." Kristy let her voice trail off and shot me a puzzled look. I'd told my friends about Mom's name change.

"Spencer. *Ms*. Spencer," I told her.

"Sorry, I forgot your new name," said Kristy.

"That's all right," Mom told her. "Why don't you all call me Maureen. It's easier."

"Okay, Maureen," I said.

"Not you!" Mom said, laughing. "My name is still the same as far as you're concerned. And it's never changing. It's Mom."

"Um . . . uh . . . Maureen," Claudia said, "I know Stacey has first dibs on a job at your store, but if you need any more help I'd love to work for you."

"I'm glad you mentioned that, Claudia. My accountant says I can't hire underage help in the store. It's against child labor laws. Though since Stacey is my daughter, I might be able to let her work a limited number of hours. But I was thinking I might like to hire you in another way."

"How?" Claudia asked.

"I'd like to contact local artists — jewelry designers, hand painters of clothing, clothing designers — and see if I can feature their products as well as more commercial clothing. I love the hand-painted shirts you make."

"And her jewelry is awesome," Mallory added.

"That too," Mom agreed. "If you want to assemble some of your things, I could look them over. We'd come to an agreement about price. I'd take a percentage and give you the rest. If that's all right with your parents, of course. I'd have to talk to them."

Claudia's face shone. "Imagine me, with my own product line. An actual working artist."

"Claudia's Funky Petunia Designs," Mary Anne suggested.

"That's it! That is totally it!" Claudia cried.

"Maureen, even if we don't work in the store, I'd be glad to help," Mallory said. "You should think about having your own Web site."

"I wouldn't know where to begin."

"I could help you," Mallory said. "Setting up a Web site is something I've been wanting to learn. The Stoneybrook Community Center is offering a course in it this summer and my parents said I could take it."

Mom grinned at her. "I'm not even in business yet and I have my own computer consultant. Wonderful!"

"We can make fliers for you and hand them out," Kristy said.

"Great! Now I have my own head of advertising too."

"I can bring the fliers to dance class with me," Jessi volunteered.

"You could also make up a computer mailing list," Mary Anne said. "I could copy our client list right out of our club notebook."

"I could help you set it up on the computer," Mallory offered. "There's a program that helps you do all that."

"Thank you, girls," Mom said. "It's terrific to know I already have such a capable team behind me."

"Are you kidding?" Kristy said. "This is the most exciting thing that's happened around here since . . .

since . . . since we started the Baby-sitters Club."

We all laughed at that. "Mom, I bought you a special gift to celebrate." I dug into the brown paper grocery bag I'd set on the counter. I pulled out a small can of anchovies.

Mom laughed. "Oh, that's okay. You don't have to do that."

"I want to. In fact, I'm going to have a piece my-self. I'll try it, anyway."

"Me too," Claudia said.

"So will I," added Mallory.

"I'm impressed," said Mom.

"Hey," I said, pulling the lid off of the anchovy can, "you have to keep changing and trying new things, right? Otherwise you'll never know what good stuff you might be missing."

About the Author

Ann Matthews Martin was born on August 12, 1955. She grew up in Princeton, NJ, with her parents and her younger sister, Jane.

Although Ann used to be a teacher and then an editor of children's books, she's now a full-time writer. She gets ideas for her books from many different places. Some are based on personal experiences. Others are based on childhood memories and feelings. Many are written about contemporary problems or events.

All of Ann's characters, even the members of the Baby-sitters Club, are made up. (So is Stoneybrook.) But many of her characters are based on real people. Sometimes Ann names her characters after people she knows; other times she chooses names she likes.

In addition to the Baby-sitters Club books, Ann Martin has written many other books for children. Her favorite is *Ten Kids, No Pets* because she loves big families and she loves animals. Her favorite BSC book is *Kristy's Big Day.* (Kristy is her favorite baby-sitter.)

Ann M. Martin now lives in New York with her cats, Gussie, Woody, and Willy, and her dog, Sadie. Her hobbies are reading, sewing, and needlework — especially making clothes for children.

Look for #11

WELCOME HOME, MARY ANNE

"Whoa," I heard Dawn say under her breath. "Sunny's good, isn't she?"

I could hardly answer. She was so good it was scaring me. I could have spent every day for a month at the pool without a guy approaching me. But all Sunny had to do was smile and make eye contact. It was as if some force field were around her that drew guys in.

"Hey," said Cole, sitting down next to Sunny.

"Hey," Sunny replied. "What's up?"

"The sun." Cole grinned.

"Funny you should mention that. That's my name. Sunny."

"I'm Cole."

"And this is Dawn, and *this*," Sunny said, pausing significantly, "is Mary Anne." She gestured toward me as if I were some precious jewel she were showing off.

"I know you." Cole gave me a closer look. "Don't you go out with that guy Logan Bruno? He's a pretty good ballplayer."

"I used to," I said.

Cole nodded. "Cool."

Sunny gave me a Look.

Cole hung around for awhile. And by the time he left, he'd asked if the three of us wanted to go to a movie that weekend, with him and two of his friends. I would have hesitated, but Sunny? She said yes before I could say a word.

And I didn't want to put a damper on her enthusiasm. After all, she was here to heal and move on. If that meant I had to go to the movies with a bunch of boys I hardly knew, who was I to say no? I wanted Sunny to be happy.